The Drop

Iohamil Navarro Cuesta

Published by UriArte Publishing & Consulting, 2024.

THE DROP

Second edition. March 29, 2024

The characters and events portrayed in this book are fictional. Any similarity to real people, living or dead, is coincidental and not intended by the author.

No part of this book may be reproduced, stored in a retrieval system, or transmitted in any form or by any means, electronic, mechanical, photocopying, recording, or otherwise, without the express written permission of the publisher.

Author: Iohamil Navarro Cuesta.

Cover illustrator: Jorge López

Translators: Majel Reyes and Jessica Van Riper

Managing editor: Jesús A. Uriarte

Copyright © 2024 Iohamil Navarro Cuesta

Published by UriArte Publishing & Consulting

Table of Contents

The Drop 1
Chapter 1 | The Attack 3
Chapter 2 | The Interrogation 13
Chapter 3 | Shaking Off the Enemy 30
Chapter 4 | Back Home 50
Chapter 5 | Friends 68
Chapter 6 | Rosa 83
Chapter 7 | The Betrayal 107
Chapter 8 | Starting Over 121

For Manuel, Hugo, Cándido, Marcos, Ageo, and many others like them,
who gave their lives for a cause that betrayed them.

> "I've had to work quietly . . ., because, to achieve certain objectives, they must be kept under cover . . ."
> José Martí

Chapter 1
The Attack

The heavy silence of the dawn annoyed him. Laying on the small couch in the living room, he kept tossing and turning hoping to fall asleep. His body felt stiff and his arms had gone numb. He stood up, picked a round cushion up off the floor and placed it on the couch. After taking off his pajama shirt and adjusting his shorts, he stretched out as much as he could. He glanced toward the back of the bungalow, into the dark bedroom, making sure that no one had been awakened by the noise. He opened the wooden blinds above the sofa and peered outside through the glass window. The light of the almost full moon sporadically pierced the thick surrounding forest and the mountains beyond it. He debated whether or not he should turn the TV back on—hoping to finally get some damned sleep.

"Better not," he muttered to himself. He knew it was a bad call.

The man went back to the couch, placed his head on the uncomfortable makeshift pillow, closed his eyes, and waited for sleep to find him. It had, or at least he thought he was dreaming, when one of the narrow panels on the bungalow's front door opened silently letting the soft porch light sneak in through the threshold. I'm definitely dreaming, he thought. The motionless shadow of a slim person dressed in dark clothes with a black weatherproof balaclava covering their face clouded the man's sleep; his nocturnal imagination confused him. The shadow took a step into the room.

"Son of a bitch," a muffled yell, nearly a murmur, escaped from his mouth.

The man leapt up off the couch like a cat and tried to grab hold of the shadow but couldn't reach it. The furtive silhouette slipped away and vanished into the darkness. He locked the door behind it and blocked it off with the small but heavy sideboard he found nearby. He rushed to the bedroom, knelt down by the bed where a woman and two small children were sleeping, and clumsily shook her awake.

"What is it, Tino?" she asked, annoyed and sleepy as she grabbed her silver Baumé & Mercier wristwatch off the nightstand; it was four thirty in the morning.

"Quickly, Claudia, get dressed. Wake the kids up."

Tino hurried to the bedroom window while Claudia hugged her children on the bed, staring at him silent and afraid. He opened the wooden blinds and slid the glass windowpane to the right. He studied the bungalow's perimeter. Everything was calm. The dim lights of the stone path that connected them to the four other bungalows were on. A sudden rustling in the branches about twenty yards away caught his attention. As soon as he located the shadow that had caused the noise, he jumped outside through the window.

"Shut the window. In about ten minutes, call the cops."

It sounded like an order rather than a request from Tino, who immediately disappeared into the darkness of the night. Claudia ran to the window, checked that each lock was secured, and returned to the bed to wake the kids just as he had instructed.

Tino crept softly and carefully through the wild vegetation following the shadow's trail. He advanced with the skill of a trained soldier, stealthily chasing his target. Cuts from the branches on his face and naked torso did not bother him, he felt he was closing in on the intruder. When he made it to the small leafy bushes that insulated a tall electric perimeter fence, he hid among them. From there he could see a cast iron gate topped with two lamps illuminating a metal sign that read Los Soles Inn. The gate was closed and its manual controls destroyed, as were the CCTV cameras that protected the entrance to the premises. The parallel rows of lights along the path continued beyond the entrance until they reached the road. Unhurried, the intruder skillfully climbed the ten-foot fence and sat at the top by the sign, preparing for his descent on the other side. He looked around. There was total silence despite having been discovered just a few minutes earlier in the bungalow. He placed his left foot on one of the fence bars and began to climb down.

Tino took off at full speed and in one leap made it halfway up the fence. He propelled himself to the top and, with only the bars between them, came face to face with the intruder, who was inevitably shocked. The man hurried down but Tino was already on the other side, and he jumped off, letting his full weight fall on the man's neck to prevent him from escaping. They both plummeted to the ground with a thud. Regaining his posture, Tino pushed a bare knee against his throat, barely letting him breathe. He yanked off the balaclava and stared him straight in the eyes.

"*¿Quién te envió?*" he asked, convinced that it had not been a random robbery attempt. "Who sent you?" This time he asked in English but was certain he wouldn't get an answer.

He knew the man had understood. He looked up for a minute and scanned the surroundings for accomplices as his knee pushed down a little harder and the stranger's face became flushed. He was trying to break free, but it was impossible. Tino's immobilization technique was flawless, and any movement he made used up the little oxygen that flowed through his body—he either breathed in a little air or choked trying. Tino returned his gaze to the immobilized body and lifted his leg. The intruder, who was about to faint, coughed in relief forcing his chest abruptly forward. Tino went behind him and grabbed his jaw with his left hand while firmly steadying his head with his right. With a sudden ninety-degree twist, the man's neck snapped immediately. Tino let his lifeless body drop to the ground.

"Groom, ready for your party?"

Tino grew still when he heard the question coming from what sounded like a walkie-talkie. He searched the only pocket in the intruder's pants, which was closed with a thick zipper. After pulling the device out, he continued searching the pocket but found nothing else. He looked around for some sort of wireless transmitter—no luck. He cautiously walked back to the bushes along the path to camouflage himself and waited a couple of seconds.

"Groom?" asked the now concerned voice.

Tino prepared himself and held the button on the walkie-talkie. "The groom stays," he said and waited for a reaction.

The lights of a car parked on the road near the inn's driveway went on as soon as the message was transmitted, and the vehicle sped away. Tino stood up and watched the car until it disappeared down a dark curve. Police car sirens could now be heard, getting increasingly louder, as they headed toward the Los Soles Inn.

The sound of the police sirens seeped in through the thick windowpanes. Tino was gazing at downtown Montreal from a tall building. All the nearby roofs were beginning to turn white, as were the streets. The snowfall was light but constant, and very visible due to the early nightfall. He listened patiently to something on the phone. He wasn't pleased by what he heard but had no intention of arguing. The typical hotel phone with its short cable didn't allow him much room, so he barely moved.

He did a quick mental count of all the police cars lined up to manage the traffic to Bell Centre, where, on giant exterior screens, a hockey game was being advertised. The Canadiens would be playing, the local favorites comparable only to his revered Industriales in the Cuban baseball league. He enjoyed the atmosphere because, regardless of the game, the residents of Montreal were loyal fans like himself, and downtown was turned upside down before and after the game. Tino took his hand to his chest, having felt his cell phone vibrate with an incoming text. He pulled out a gray iPhone 6 and read the message.

"I have to go downstairs, they're waiting for me," he explained in a conciliatory tone. "Claudia? Claudia?"

Frustrated, he hung up the phone, returned the cell phone to his jacket pocket, and headed toward the door. Before exiting, he adjusted his tie in the mirror on the wall of the narrow hallway.

The lobby of the Sheraton was buzzing with tourists drinking all sorts of alcoholic beverages. They made predictions on the hockey game and interrupted the first relaxing drink of the evening for the businessmen sitting at the bar, who had returned to the hotel after a tiring workday. Tino headed straight for the last table, where two people were seated.

"Sorry for the delay, Rosa. They haven't arrived yet?" he asked as he sat down at the table.

"No, but they should be here any minute," she replied. "What time is it, Miguel?"

Miguel checked the silver Omega on his left wrist as he took a sip of Jack Daniels on the rocks from a heavy crystal glass.

"Six o'clock," he answered. "Do you want anything?" he asked Tino.

"Yes please."

Miguel made a practiced gesture, signaling for the waiter to come over. The waiter knew them and approached the table in less than ten seconds; he addressed Tino right away.

"*Cuba Libre*?" the waiter asked, confident that he had guessed correctly.

"No, not today. Make it a seven-year Havana Club, neat."

He had not yet finished his order, and the waiter was already headed for the bar. Rosa scanned the place expecting someone to show up when the Blackberry on the table next to the water bottle started ringing. She gazed at the phone sensing what the call was about, but she didn't move until it stopped ringing. It rang again, and this time she did pick it up.

"Hello?" she answered in English with a steady voice. She listened for a moment and hung up. Angry, she grabbed the water bottle and stood up: "Today's meeting has been canceled." She pondered for a second. "Fuck them. We're going back to Cuba."

The two men were shocked by the drastic order. Tino didn't question her decision but Miguel, on the other hand, tried to conceal his disagreement. The waiter returned with the drink and interrupted the awkward moment. He put the glass on the table and left, getting lost in the crowded lobby.

"We still have time, Rosa," Miguel said while checking his watch again. "I can establish contact with my agent in the government before we do something that could be irreversible. I don't think they made us come all the way here just to stand us up. Do you?"

Miguel pulled out his cell phone and held it as he waited for her response. Rosa remained standing, unaffected by Miguel's pressure. She took a small sip of water straight from the bottle and stared at them.

"How long have the three of us been working together?" she asked, already knowing the answer.

Miguel and Tino were unsure as to why she would ask that. They looked at each other puzzled, not knowing how to answer.

"Including the period of my predecessor," she clarified, to relieve the pressure.

"Ten years," Tino said.

"Exactly. Long enough to get to know me and know that I won't make the same mistake that cost him his job. What we're experiencing now is the new Cold War, but unlike the one I lived through in the '80s and '90s—which you only know from history books—in this one as long as I'm the boss of this department the three of us will be taking the analogue route because there's no way digitalization is going to fuck me over."

The silence was absolute.

"Well, at least our new Russian allies aren't very tech savvy," joked Tino, hoping to ease the tension.

The joke was not met with the reception he expected. Rosa stood there, motionless, while Miguel put his cell back in his pocket.

"*Da, tovarishch*," she confirmed in perfect Russian. "Despite all their flaws, they are the best allies we've got right now."

With those words she concluded her unexpected scolding, certain that her comments had achieved the calming effect she was aiming for. Just then, the vibration of Tino's cell phone made him instinctively reach for his interior jacket pocket to check the text. He was about to pull it out but hesitated with Rosa staring at him.

"Aren't you going to answer it?" she asked him harshly.

He did not hesitate to accept his boss's challenge and pulled the phone out. Miguel quietly enjoyed this moment between the two of them. He savored every drop of his Jack Daniels trying to forget the scolding he'd received seconds earlier. Tino glanced at the text casually without giving it much importance.

"It's Claudia. Again," he huffed in frustration and put the phone back in his pocket.

Rosa smiled mockingly. "Just grant her the divorce Tino, trust me. You'll feel better when she is not bugging you every minute of the day," her voice was almost maternal.

"I've already agreed. As soon as we get back from our vacation in Spain at the end of next month, I'll sign the papers."

Pleased by the answer, Rosa turned around and headed to the elevator in the lobby without saying goodbye. Tino took a long sip of his Havana Club as he pulled out his iPhone again. He affectionately looked at the picture of his children on the screen.

"I'm sorry about the divorce."

The comment struck him. He waited a couple of seconds before replying.

"Thanks, Miguel. It's the best thing for everyone," he said with resignation and placed his cell on the table.

Miguel looked down at the picture of the kids. "Why don't you come with me to Saint Catherine's club?" he asked, trying to cheer him up.

"What the fuck, Miguel? I'm not in the mood for whores today. I think I'd better go to the Canadiens game and pretend I'm in the Latino cheering for the Industriales, at least I'll burn off some energy."

"Man, the scalpers must be charging a fortune today. I know money is no issue for you but we're not talking about the World Series here. Where will you find a ticket less than an hour before the game starts?"

"At Pietro's bar, across from Bell Centre."

Miguel frowned with concern when he heard the name of the place. It wasn't the answer he was expecting.

"Are you out of your mind?" he said in a patronizing tone. "You're giving yourself away, putting yourself in the lion's den for nothing. An Italian-owned bar in Montreal is a definite FBI hangout. That place must be loaded with mics and cameras—"

"Don't worry so much, we all know each other anyways," interrupted Tino. "*Dale*, see you in Havana," he said as he stood up, grabbed his cell phone from the table, and headed to the elevator, leaving Miguel by himself.

Wearing his blue Industriales baseball cap, Tino joined the group of fans walking from the Sheraton Hotel to the Bell Centre along René Lévesque Street, cheering with the best of them. Thanks to their winter garments the group looked uniform in color, except for those who defied the cold and left their torsos uncovered due to the effects of all kinds of substances. Tino was not bothered by the harsh Montreal winter, he felt at ease with the exception of one thing—the salt used in cities like Montreal to keep the snow from turning into ice. He had decided to walk the three blocks that separated the hotel from the Bell Centre without using the Underground City tunnels that so conveniently enabled locals to have a social life despite the low temperatures. On the way back, when the cold would be more intense, and the salt on the sidewalks and the street would have turned into a disgusting sludge, then he would take the underground network.

Pietro's Bar, across the street from the Bell Centre, was packed. Fans were piling up both inside and out. He made his way in, trying not to be too much of a disturbance. Alcohol was having a negative effect on the crowd and fights were constantly breaking out among the fans. Not without effort, he reached the bar and made a spot for himself among the other customers as best he could.

A burly, bald man walked toward him from the other end of the bar. Tino stared at him intently, taking a black iPhone from his left pants pocket. He typed and sent a very short message and placed the phone among the bottles and glasses piling up on the bar. Now facing Tino, the man placed a dark square coaster next to the iPhone. He grabbed a bottle of seven-year Havana Club from on top of one of the refrigerators, poured some rum into a small clear glass, and placed it on the coaster.

"Thanks, Pietro," Tino said and drank the rum in one gulp. He then placed the empty glass on top of the cell phone and took the coaster placing it in the left pocket of his pants. He turned around and headed for the door. Pietro followed him with his eyes until he was gone. As soon as he left, Pietro started to clear the bar full of empty bottles and glasses—Tino's phone among them.

The end of the hockey game between the Canadiens and the Washington Capitals was playing on television. Just behind the Canadiens' goal, Rosa could see Tino wearing his inseparable blue Industriales cap, singing away and hugging the fans, celebrating the Canadiens' victory over their archenemy. The game was over, and the crowd was beginning to leave the Bell Centre. The sound of police sirens once again could be heard through the thick windowpanes of the rooms at the Sheraton hotel.

Chapter 2
The Interrogation

The Skoda car belonging to the Spanish Civil Guard blocked the driveway to Los Soles Inn about six feet from the entrance gate. Dawn was breaking and daylight had already begun to illuminate the area. Barefoot and still in his pajama shorts, Tino was leaning against the front of the car watching a young and inexperienced agent walk in circles, over and over again, around the intruder's corpse. Curiosity and nausea permeated his examination and prevented him from getting too close to the body. Inside the car, another agent, who seemed more experienced in dealing with the criminal world, paid no attention to the deceased, chatting away on his cell to kill some time as they waited on the police examiners. Tino slowly paced back and forth, interrupting the rookie's concentration now and then.

"You think it will be much longer before the examiners arrive?" he asked. "I want to let my wife know that I'm okay."

"They should be here soon. Don't worry, we've already contacted her and told her that you're safe, with us," he emphasized. "We've asked her to wait for you in the bungalow."

Tino accepted the explanation with resignation. As he was leaning on the car, he noticed the intruder's wireless transmitter, camouflaged on the similarly colored soil, a few steps away from the agent. He approached him with confidence.

"Do you know him, Menéndez?" he asked, reading the name tag displayed on his uniform.

Tino crouched down by the man's head. Menéndez had no time to question his audacity and couldn't help but smile at the question as he squatted down next to him.

"No way, man! This *guiri* could be from anywhere but here."

"*Guiri?*"

"Yeah, in Andalusia that's what we call white foreigners like him who come here to get burnt to a crisp in the sun. Apparently, this one didn't get the chance to."

Tino looked up when he heard the experts' minivan approaching. It had reached the edge of the road and was headed toward them. He stood up and took a step backwards, covering the transmitter with his left foot. He grabbed it with his toes and walked back to the police car while the agent finished up his phone call to go and greet the experts. Seeing them arrive, Menéndez stood up and adjusted his uniform, ready to brief them. As he headed for the vehicle, he stopped next to Tino.

"What did I tell you?" he said proudly. "As soon as they are done questioning you, you can return to your family.

The water fell hard on the shower floor mixing in with the steam generated by the temperature difference. The clear glass door that separated it from the rest of the bathroom was open, allowing the water to splash onto Tinos's feet—which were dirty, scratched, and showing traces of blood. Standing in front of the large white sink, he wiped the moisture off the mirror and steadied his gaze on it. He was focused, trying to organize his thoughts, not paying any attention to the scratches on his face. He activated the faucet sensor and water started pouring out immediately. He did the same thing with the soap dispenser hanging under the mirror and began to scrub his fingertips to remove the ink that was left from when the experts took his fingerprints. As he did, he glanced over to the left side of the sink where he had placed the intruder's walkie-talkie and wireless transmitter.

The water turned off automatically and he quickly dried his hands. He grabbed the radio and deftly slid the back cover off, looking for any inscription or lettering that would give away its origin, but he found none. He removed the battery and tossed it into the toilet to his left. Same with the transmitter, both objects fell to the bottom of the spotless white bowl. He opened the mirror that served as a door to a well-stocked and brightly lit medicine cabinet. Inside it sat a medium-sized brown suede case with fine dark lines. After taking it out, he placed it on the right side of the sink. He opened the zipper displaying a neatly arranged Gillette disposable razor, a small container of Gillette shaving gel, and the coaster he had collected at Pietro's the night of the Canadiens game. He flipped it over and from the back of the coaster he pulled out a black iPhone 6 and a small sky-blue USB flash drive that had been embedded in the cork and added them to the other objects. He looked up, searching for something else in the cabinet. He took out a disposable syringe still wrapped in plastic, broke the seal, and carefully held the needle.

He turned on the cell phone, checked that the inbox was empty, and turned it off. With surgical precision, he inserted the needle tip into the SIM card hole to eject it. The card was matte white and had no letters or numbers on it. He lifted it to eye level and studied it under the cabinet lights before crushing it against the sink, breaking it into several pieces that joined the other objects at the bottom of the toilet. Turning his attention back to the items on his right, he now focused on the flash drive.

The kids were running around the few pieces of furniture in the bungalow's living room. The red lights on the soles of their white sneakers flashed with every step. The sideboard that had been used a few hours ago to block the entrance was now back in its original position and the door was wide open. Sitting on the couch, anxiously waiting on Tino, Claudia mechanically counted the three suitcases by the door, ready to be shipped off again. She tried not to think too much about events of the night before or the reason for their sudden departure. Tino came out of the bedroom already dressed, clean shaven with a few improvised bandages on his face, and carrying a dark blue backpack on his shoulder. He checked his pants pockets to make sure he had his necessary personal belongings: keys, phone, wallet. Lastly, he touched his left wrist to confirm that he was wearing his blue Casio Shock watch.

"All set?" he asked Claudia, knowing she was. Without waiting for an answer, he turned to the children: "Lucas, Rafael, we're leaving!"

Claudia shot him a wordless glance by way of reply while the kids kept playing. Tino put on his backpack and took a suitcase in each hand. Claudia had just stood up to get the third one when agent Menéndez arrived at the door. His presence made her uncomfortable. Seeing him, the kids stopped playing and approached their mother, their annoying shoe lights had finally stopped going off.

"Will you lend me a hand with the suitcase, please?" Tino addressed Menéndez right away to prevent him from interacting with the rest of his family. He knew that this untimely visit was not a coincidence.

Menéndez had no choice but to comply with his request. He greeted Claudia with a nod as she clutched her children tightly against her body. He grabbed the suitcase and walked with Tino toward the car.

The agent's car was parked next to a Mercedes-Benz GLC 300. Tino pressed the key fob and the trunk opened automatically. He placed the two suitcases inside and waited for the agent with a smile that was not reciprocated. Menendez ignored Tino's gesture to take the suitcase and placed it next to the other two himself.

"Alberto Urrutia, the head of the Task Force, is already at the precinct. As you requested, he is waiting for you there."

"Thank you," Tino replied.

Menéndez went to leave but Tino grabbed him by the arm, which he immediately released to avoid any misunderstanding.

"I don't want my family to have anything to do with this. My wife is easily upset by these things and the kids, you know, they're kids."

His words had the sympathetic effect he'd wanted. Menéndez relaxed and it showed in his body language.

"Of course, I understand. We didn't tell her about the deceased when we contacted her. How old are the kids?" he asked with interest.

"The oldest, Lucas, is six and Rafa, four."

Tino pressed the button to lock the trunk, which slowly closed. Out of the corner of his eye, he saw Claudia and the children walking toward them.

"I'm going to drop them in Ronda, and I'll go to the precinct right after," he added.

He said goodbye to Menéndez with a brief handshake, and the agent went straight to his patrol car. Tino walked over to the kids, picked them both up in his arms and began spinning around like a top as Claudia got into the car. The children's laughter successfully distracted him from the difficult moment. He put them back on the ground and instantly their shoe lights started going off again, causing him to wince in disapproval—Who the hell came up with the idea of putting lights in shoes? he wondered.

The gentle slope of the stretch of Ronda Boulevard that led to the precinct was crowded with tourists and their inseparable counterpart, vendors. Tino scanned for gaps between them where he'd be able to take at least a few steps in a row before stopping and finding the next open spot. There was always a human or material obstacle: a lamp post, a traffic sign, or a trash can. He spotted the police station roof thanks to the Spanish military flag waving on top of it. He was almost there.

During the hectic walk, he tried to identify who was watching him within the tide of people crowding the street. He was certain that someone was tailing him. He took advantage of a brief stop at a crosswalk to discreetly remove the black iPhone 6 from his pocket. The crosswalk light changed and a human avalanche propelled him across the street, back onto the boulevard, in a matter of seconds. He plunged into the crowd of visitors once again, spotted a small space next to a dumpster, and made his way there. He dropped his cell phone inside before immediately joining a group of Brits who had just finished the morning leg of their guided tour and were on their way to the parking lot—strategically located at the beginning of the boulevard.

Tino waited patiently in Alberto Urrutia's small office, seated in an uncomfortable wooden chair on the back of which rested his backpack. The air conditioning was very cold and the sunlight coming in through the balcony, with glass panes and no curtains, had no effect on the room's temperature whatsoever. Tino thoroughly scanned the office. In front of him, a worn wooden desk housed a telephone and an HP computer, accompanied only by the remote control for the AC, which had been arranged perfectly perpendicular to the monitor. A completely impersonal environment, with no papers or personal mementos. A regular black office chair tilted farther back than usual, probably due to the weight of its usual occupant, was hidden under the desk. Behind it, there was the omnipresent photo of His Majesty King Felipe VI.

And they say that only Cubans are slaves to cults of personality, he thought as he grabbed the AC control to raise the temperature to 77 degrees, making it cut off. He put the remote back beside the computer.

Every wall was lined with old shelves crammed with files that could barely accommodate the hundreds of papers. The office door remained closed, and although Tino heard a few isolated voices, he didn't care to know what they were saying. He checked the time on his watch, it had been twenty-five minutes since his arrival at the police station. The office door suddenly opened.

"I'm sorry for the delay."

Tino stood up facing the impressive figure of a man in civilian clothes who was a foot taller than him, and twice his age and heftiness.

"Don't worry about it," he said and shook his hand.

"Alberto Urrutia, nice to meet you. Please, sit down."

Urrutia went straight to his desk, pushed back the chair, and dropped his full body weight down on it. He placed a sealed yellow envelope next to the computer as Tino sat back down in his seat. Urrutia glanced at the AC remote that was out of place. He read something on the computer screen, typed a few words, and slid the monitor to the side so that they could face each other without anything between them. He held the envelope in his hand but did not open it, ready to begin the informal interrogation.

"I turned up the temperature a bit. It was very cold," Tino said before the officer could mention it.

"I've been here for two years and I still can't get used to this damned heat," he said, a little annoyed by the unexpected audacity.

"Where are you from originally? Basque, right?" asked Tino, convinced that he was correct.

"San Sebastian," the other man answered proudly, and turned the AC back on. "I'm very sorry for what happened. Believe me, it's the first time something this serious has taken place at one of our inns. Los Soles is one of the most luxurious in the area," he emphasized as he adjusted the temperature to his liking.

"Let's hope it's the first and the last," Tino replied.

Urrutia smiled in agreement and pointed to the cuts on his face. "Everything all right?"

Tino brushed his injuries aside and Urrutia let it go, continuing his line of inquiry.

"Your wife and children are still unaware of everything, right?"

"That's right, and I'd rather keep it that way if you don't mind."

The officer nodded without hesitation. Finally, he opened the envelope and took out a small bundle of papers.

"Celestino Font Lavandero," he read slowly.

Tino remained silent, awaiting his next comment. Urrutia looked up, meeting his eyes directly, and Tino did not look away.

"You hardly ever hear that name in this country anymore, Celestino—"

"My grandfather," he promptly explained. He began to think that the interview was going to take longer than he had anticipated.

"How convenient," he commented with some irony.

"In my family, we are all descendants of Spaniards."

"I don't doubt it, if I had met you anywhere else, I'd think you were Spanish, not Cuban."

Tino was not pleased with the tone of the conversation, and it did not go unnoticed.

"How rude of me! Would you like some water or anything else to drink? In this heat . . . " He lifted the receiver and dialed a number as he waited for an answer from Tino, who, instead, turned around and produced a bottle of water from one of his backpack's side pockets. The officer hung up and said jokingly, "Tourists, always ready."

Tino intentionally did not react to the joke. Urrutia picked up the first sheet of paper from the pile, which displayed the passport photo of a younger Tino, and showed it to him. He realized that the officer had done his homework before the interview.

"From your first trip to Spain, right?" he asked.

"Yes," Tino responded tersely.

"How old were you then?"

The question was totally unnecessary, but he decided to play along as part of his strategy.

"I'd better give you the whole story, that way we don't miss anything. What do you say?"

"Please."

The officer dropped the envelope onto his desk and leaned back in his chair without taking his eyes off Tino.

"I was twenty-five, had just graduated from college, and was placed at the Cuban Embassy in Madrid; Cuba needed to have English translators on hand to move them between Europe and Africa as needed. I thought it was a great way to get to see the world. I worked from there for the next four years until I went back to Cuba. I had the chance to learn a lot about everything, which helped me land a job at the Ministry of Foreign Trade where I still happily work."

His tone of voice could not have been more dense or flat. He even bored himself with his story. Urrutia leaned forward against the desk and grabbed the envelope once more.

"Very good summary. However, you left out something rather relevant. At least, in my opinion." He looked for a specific piece of paper in the bundle. "In our files from six years ago, your name appears in connection with a serious traffic accident that happened in broad daylight on Madrid's Gran Via. Miraculously, you were unharmed but the person in the other car regretfully passed away. I found out a lot of information about the accident because the man who died was a

Bulgarian citizen." He stopped to read the sheet of paper: "Viktor Stoickov, NATO liaison for Eastern Europe."

He looked back at Tino, whose calm and disinterested attitude was unwavering.

"This other guy"—Urrutia pulled out a different page with a picture of the intruder's corpse and showed it to Tino, who did not flinch—"looks like Viktor, European, in his thirties, I don't think I could ever forget something like that, the nightmares would haunt me. Don't you have nightmares, Celestino?" he asked him.

Tino maintained his composure as he listened. He remembered the events perfectly.

"These things happen in life, and one prefers to forget them. We were both in the wrong place at the wrong time," he claimed, fully in control.

Urrutia was not convinced by his answer and remained quiet, prompting him to elaborate further.

"I'm sure a man like you, with your age and proven experience doesn't work at this precinct by choice. There must be some godforsaken reason for you to finish out your career in the ass end of Andalusia chasing pickpockets and petty thieves," Tino retorted sarcastically.

The officer took offense and could not hide his discomfort.

"How does a person fall from a fence that's barely ten feet high and break his neck so easily? Here is something that might help you with your answer—the only two times you've been in Spain, years apart," Urrutia insisted, "you've been involved in two *accidental* deaths. I'd say the odds of that happening to the same person are very low. Strange, don't you think?" he asked.

Tino agreed with him, but it didn't matter anymore. He had managed to get to where he wanted sooner than expected. Urrutia's soft laughter revealed more anxiety than joy. He was eager to provoke him.

"The man got scared when he saw me and lost his balance. He just landed badly." He made it simple knowing there were no witnesses or evidence from the actual events. He was poking at the other man's discomfort.

"And don't you find it very irresponsible of you to chase after a thief in the middle of the night in an unfamiliar place?" the officer interjected, trusting his own judgment.

Tino was smiling on the inside. He had predicted Urrutia's questioning almost word for word. He settled back in his chair to conceal his reaction.

"When his children are in danger, a father is capable of anything. Wouldn't you do the same for yours?" he asked.

He worried that his statement had perhaps been too obvious, although he was confident that his question wouldn't let Urrutia read too far into his words beyond the context of the situation at hand. He was trying to confirm his theory about the old officer's loneliness.

"I don't have children but yes, I'm almost certain I'd have done the same," he answered with resignation.

Tino was silent. His assumption had been correct. Urrutia went back to flipping through the papers, then paused at one and looked him straight in the eye.

"According to your statement, the thief barely made it past the entrance door. You were sleeping on the couch and you startled him before he could come in. So why put your family at risk by leaving them alone?"

Tino realized he had made a mistake underestimating him.

"Instinct. As I said, if you were a father you'd understand," he insisted, pushing the topic of the officer's lack of family. Urrutia had a fine poker face and pretended that he hadn't taken the bait.

Tino looked at his watch to appear restless, just to throw the officer off. He couldn't afford another mistake. The sturdy man went through the file once again, taking his time.

"Although you came as a tourist, you are currently traveling with a diplomatic passport," he stated, directing his gaze to the bottle of water that Tino still held in his hands.

"Yes, as I told you, the ministry I work for requires me to travel with that passport."

Urrutia smiled slightly, preparing himself for the next question as he looked back at the papers. He gathered them together and placed them back in the envelope, which he carefully closed before putting it aside. He crossed his thick fingers interlocking his hands, ready for anything.

"Forgive my ignorance, but as far as I know the Cuban communist government pays its employees very poorly. Yet, Celestino, you drive a new Mercedes, stayed in the fanciest hotel in Ronda, and have been touring Andalusia for a week. And who knows where else you'll go, Barcelona perhaps?" he said sarcastically.

Tino thought it was much too easy of a way to end the interview. He was not going to fall into the trap of a political debate about Cuba, its government, or its integrity. It wasn't worth taking up the extra time. Claudia must have been restlessly awaiting his return. The moment had arrived to put pressure on Urrutia, and Tino was confident that he would come out on top. He stood up, picked up his backpack from the back of the chair, and intentionally left the empty bottle on Urrutia's desk. He strapped on his backpack while the officer remained seated, in defiance.

"It's true, civil servants don't have good salaries. My wife's name is Claudia Sureda, as in the Suredas from Barcelona, who everyone knows. But I'm sure you already knew that."

He headed for the door. Urrutia stood up and they reached the doorway at the same time. The officer opened it but blocked the exit with his arm.

"You're very lucky. Despite your diplomatic status, I'm asking you to please stay in touch with us. I've ordered the autopsy and would like to share the results with you before you leave Spain. Understood?" he asked in a threatening tone.

Tino smiled.

"You know very well what the procedure is in these situations. If you want to talk to me, get in touch with my embassy," he replied in the same tone.

He stared at the arm that was preventing him from leaving. Urrutia had no choice but to let him go. Tino extended his hand to say goodbye and the other followed his lead reluctantly, knowing it was very likely he'd never see him again.

Tino took a different route on his way back to meet Claudia and the kids in the center of Ronda. The side streets off the main boulevard were nearly deserted, with very few tourists, aside from those who had opted against the popular attractions and had instead gone in search of local authenticity. He had also chosen that way to force his pursuer to expose himself. He walked under the shade of the awnings that covered bar and restaurant entrances, mainly frequented by local residents. The midday sun was relentless, just like in Cuba. He made a quick stop at a bar, opened the small fridge by the entrance, and grabbed the coldest bottle of water.

The bar's regulars chatted loudly as if they were in their own living rooms. He looked around to spot the waiter, and when he did, he held up the two-euro coin that was in his left hand and placed it on the counter. He went back outside, stood under the awning, and took a long sip of water to quench his thirst. He then took a couple of steps into the middle of the street, glanced toward one corner then the next, and smoothly dropped his backpack off his back, grabbing it by the handle. He was showing off in front of his pursuer.

Claudia sat at a patio table outside a restaurant while Lucas and Rafael played in front of her, running around the water fountain set in the center of the plaza. On the table, a pitcher of Sangria was sweating in the heat, though both glasses remained untouched. In one corner of the table, there were two plates stacked one on top of the other to protect the food inside. Most of the visitors were seeking refuge from the sun, tucked into the adjacent establishments. Claudia preferred to sit outside, that way she could keep a close eye on her kids while they were having fun.

The sun was shining so brightly on the plaza that the lights on the children's shoes were barely visible, not that she really missed them. There were very few people out at the time, and she easily spotted Tino as he appeared on the other end of the plaza and headed directly for his sons. He briefly greeted them before joining her at the table. With a tired gesture, he tossed the backpack onto a chair and sat next to her so that he could also watch the kids. After pouring Sangria into both glasses, he downed his in one gulp.

"Sorry, it took longer than I expected at the station."

Claudia did not pay much attention to his explanation. She wasn't interested in the details.

"Has the thief been arrested?" she asked.

"Not yet, but I already pressed charges so we can get on with our trip."

Tino did not take his eyes off the children. His wife, free from the pressure of constantly watching over them, began to relax as she drank her sangria.

"What about the chair?"

"What chair?" he replied with another question, knowing exactly what she meant.

"The chair you always put behind the front door wherever we spend the night when we're not at home. Didn't it make a noise when the thief opened the door?"

"I forgot to do it," he said to Claudia's surprise—she did not buy his confession.

"Have you eaten?" he asked, turning his head slightly to look at her and changing the subject.

She nodded and he returned his gaze to the boys.

"Your food is probably cold by now," she remarked.

Tino leaned forward to grab the plates. He removed the one on top and taking a look at the assortment of tapas decided to go for the tuna stuffed peppers. He ate them both in one bite.

"What time do you think we'll make it to Barcelona? I want to let Mom know so that she can be at the hotel waiting for us," his wife asked.

Tino was still eating, he was hungry.

"The hotel reservation in Barcelona is for today, right?"

The question gave her pause. "It is, because when I made it, you assured me that we'd be getting there today. Why?"

"We'll get there tomorrow."

Claudia grabbed her purse to look for her cell phone.

"Don't worry, I'll call the hotel to let them know—"

He stopped her, placing his hand on her arm.

"Okay, well, where are we spending the night?" she asked him, no longer looking for her cell.

"In Cordova. I want us to visit the Triumph of San Raphael. You'll like it, you'll see."

"Why the change of plans?" Claudia was not sure she wanted to know the answer.

"To shake off the enemy," he said jokingly with a mischievous smile.

"I'm not in the mood for jokes. Have you been to Cordova before?" She showed no signs of discontent about the sudden change of plans because, actually, it did not bother her. On the contrary, she thought it was a good idea.

"Yes, once, when I lived here."

They both drank from their glasses. Tino seemed calmer and more relaxed; he enjoyed the sight of his children playing in the unforgiving Andalusian sun.

"Why don't we just stay and live in Spain once and for all?"

The question took him by surprise. Disrupting the peaceful moment they had both been enjoying.

"We've already talked about this. I cannot and will not live here," he answered sharply.

"You and your goddamn job and your goddamn responsibility to Cuba. The kids and I always come last. That's what really pisses me off."

He paused before replying. He didn't like arguing with her, especially when she was right.

"My job is not the issue. Besides, you've always been on board with what I do."

"Sometimes I wish I hadn't been," she said angrily.

The silence between them lasted an eternity. Neither one wanted to take their eyes off the children. Tino stared at the bottom of his glass for a few minutes, deep in thought.

"Claudia, when we return to Cuba, I'll do as you asked and sign the divorce papers," Tino admitted.

"I don't want to . . . " Claudia made an effort to keep it together. "So, you're going to take after your mentor, even in this?" she replied, as if she were a judge delivering a sentence. "You're going to end up a lonely drunkard, just like him."

Claudia's words had an unexpected effect on him, sadly, he identified with what she had said. He slid his chair over to sit in front of her; she kept her composure and did her best to hold back the tears.

"After all these years together, it just doesn't seem fair, does it?" his wife asked.

"It's what's best for you and the kids," he conceded.

They gazed at each other without any further words. With resignation, Claudia gave in first and turned back toward the square to watch the kids. She picked up her glass and sipped her sangria. Tino immediately stood up, looking for the boys. Rafael and Lucas were talking with a middle-aged couple. He rushed over to them like a scared wild animal. Claudia sat up in her chair as she saw him take off. She got up to follow him, but he already had one boy tucked under each arm, and they were waving goodbye to the couple.

Chapter 3
Shaking Off the Enemy

The traffic on the A-4 highway was busy, but manageable. Tino drove at a leisurely pace, it was barely four in the afternoon and the highway sign indicated that the next exit for Cordova was only about a mile away. The rest of the family slept peacefully in the car, especially the kids, who were finally worn out from exhaustion. The view was beautiful, mountains and plains shared the green landscape of early spring. After passing through a mountain tunnel a few thousand yards long, he pulled off onto the shoulder to briefly stretch his legs before driving through Cordova's narrow and uneven streets. He parked without making any sudden movements and got out, leaving the door ajar so as not to wake anyone. As he walked to the back of the car, he kept track of the vehicles that were on his same route; memorizing the make, model, color, and passengers as they went by.

Cordova was not very different from Ronda, just bigger. Tourists crowded every corner and the traffic was unbearable. It wasn't worth it to drive into the city center. Finding a parking space as close as possible to the Triumph of San Raphael would do. The Andalusia Bridge was the least busy since it was located a little farther away from the tourist attractions. As they continued in the slow-moving traffic, Tino started to remember the city and its streets. Unhurried, he kept an eye out for any open parking spot. After turning left on Isasa Street he found a space, one block away, in front of a restaurant named Regadera. The spot was a tight fit, but the modern Mercedes didn't take up much room. Claudia woke up just as he was making the last turn. She settled into her seat and looked around, still sleepy.

"I'm going to book a table for tonight. Grab a couple of sweaters from the bag because it'll be nightfall before we get back," suggested Tino in a quiet voice.

Claudia looked at the place he was pointing to and thought it seemed alright, at least from the outside. He got out and she lowered the visor in front of her. The mirror lights went on automatically. She fixed her long thin blonde hair as she watched the kids, who were still napping.

The restaurant door was open even though the place was still closed. Tino made it to a small counter by the entrance where a pen and a sheet of paper filled with names and times were laid out. The kitchen, separated by a clear glass wall, was dark, and the chairs were stacked upside down on their tables. It was a rather small place. A young woman appeared in the back hallway, near the bathroom sign.

"May I help you," she asked.

"Please," he replied.

The young woman approached the counter without delay. Tino couldn't help but notice her striking honey-colored eyes that contrasted with her long black hair, pulled up in a messy ponytail.

"I'd like to reserve a table for four tonight. I've heard good things about this place."

The woman's face said it all. It appeared it would be an impossible mission to get a reservation at that time on a Saturday.

"I wish I could help you, but I don't have anything open. I'm sorry."

He was not discouraged by the bad news.

"Nothing at all? Look, I'm not very picky, I just want to have dinner..."

He was openly flirting with her, and she gave it right back to him. She kept touching her ponytail while she checked the sheet of paper over and over again trying to find a solution.

"I could book you very early, at eight, and give you the worst table we have."

She pointed to the hallway that she had emerged from minutes ago. A lonely table, half hidden by a column, seemed to be the only alternative.

"Perfect, I'm Cuban, we have dinner earlier than you guys anyway."

His reaction was genuine, it caught her by surprise—she was accustomed to dealing with clients upset over the table's location.

"Very well, then. Under what name?"

"Tino, four people, at eight o'clock."

The young woman took down the reservation in the corner of the paper and added the number 13 next to his name.

"Thank you very much."

"My pleasure," she replied expecting a line from Tino, who was already heading for the door. When he opened it, he turned around to look at her.

"Having your hair up makes you look older, older than I think you actually are," he said and waved goodbye, leaving her with a sly smile on her face.

In a single tug, she let her hair down and placed the paper and the pen back on the counter to return to her restaurant chores.

Claudia and the kids were on the sidewalk, checking out the area. The lights on the kids' shoes were flashing again, although Lucas's left sneaker kept fading out. Tino joined them and Claudia handed him his inseparable backpack, which he immediately put on.

"Well, you're the only one of us who's been here. Where to?"

He enjoyed being the head of the family and the question couldn't have been more welcomed.

"That way." He pointed east, where most tourists were headed. He waited for his wife and children to position themselves ahead of him, so that they would always walk in front.

The Triumph of San Raphael was not as sought after by tourists as the Mosque or the Alcazar of the Christian Monarchs, which made it easier for them to get to the monument. Claudia and Tino felt a connection to the place because of their son Rafael; the Triumph watched over them. The children sat on the stairs while he looked for an amateur photographer among the visitors. He spotted a local couple walking near the monument's entrance.

"Quickly, give me your phone," he said to his wife.

She reached into her pocket and handed it to him. He immediately approached the couple, addressing the man.

"Excuse me, would you mind taking our picture?" he asked.

The man smiled and took the cell phone with distinct skill.

"If I charged a peseta for every picture I took in this place, I'd be a millionaire," he muttered, making his wife laugh.

Tino returned to his family. Claudia took the opportunity to lean her body against his. From their spot, he could clearly see the opposite corner of the plaza, where the back of the Mosque was buzzing with tourists, locals, and fortune-telling gypsies.

"Please take a few, if you don't mind," he asked the man in order to buy time and further study the faces that passed him.

When the man was satisfied with his work, he stopped taking pictures. Tino went to him and took back his phone.

"I don't think you looked good in any of them. You spent the whole time fidgeting behind your wife."

"Oh, don't worry about it, I'm sure one of them will do. I really appreciate it. Can I buy you a beer?" he asked.

"No need, enjoy the walk with your family."

The man said goodbye and resumed his walk with his wife. Claudia joined Tino and checked the pictures on her phone.

"LR, we're leaving."

The children perfectly understood the meaning of the two consonants. There was no question, the tour was starting up again. This time, Tino led the kids holding their hands, one on each side, while Claudia walked a few steps ahead. As they neared the main entrance to the Mosque, gypsies rushed at her and she quickly brushed them off. Tino was not fazed by the swarm of women because Claudia was capable of defending herself. A middle-aged gypsy woman went straight to Lucas and grabbed his hand, much to Tino's annoyed surprise.

"Either you let go of his hand, or I'll break your wrist in two," he warned her emphatically.

The woman shouted and cursed but let him go without a second thought. The rest of them ignored Tino and his family and immediately moved on to their next victim.

The Mosque was a haven of peace and tranquility, with a more comfortable temperature compared to the climate outside. Most tourists respected the place for the sacred site that it was. There was no shouting, no cell phones constantly ringing, no camera flashes disturbing the intimacy of the space. As soon as they traversed the building's wide entryway, the interior opened up considerably and their eyes fell upon hundreds of tall slender columns that supported the arabesque arcs, running the length and width of the Mosque. The wealth was spread throughout the center section as well, with luxurious catholic altars plated in gold and precious wood—undoubtedly pillaged from remote lands. Very few places in the world could peacefully bring together Catholics and Muslims under the same roof to worship their respective gods in a shared space. Tino felt as though he was rediscovering the place, and Claudia took in every detail with interest and admiration for the vast ornamentation that covered every corner.

The children and Tino wandered around while Claudia headed in the opposite direction, focused on the various altars protected by security fencing. Lucas and Rafael hid behind the columns, playing among the shadows and patches of light that covered the floor. Although he was paying full attention to his kids, he could sense the intensity of his pursuer's gaze. He needed to find out who it was. Tino scanned the center of the temple pretending to look for his wife, but in reality, he was trying to identify any face that had been repeated throughout the day. Looking forward once again, his breath caught in his chest. Lucas and Rafael were gone. He could hear their voices as part of the general chatter but couldn't locate the exact spot they were coming from.

He quickened his pace, bumping into and startling other visitors. He didn't care, desperation got the better of him. He stopped in the wide hallway and crouched down with his face hovering above the floor to look for the lights coming from his sons' shoes. All around him, people on both sides of the hallway slowed to a stop due to overcrowding. Twenty yards in front of him he spotted the red flashes darting back and forth and running around the columns. He stood up, made his way through the offended tourists, and ran as fast as he could.

"Damn it!" he yelled as he was about to reach them. His exclamation stopped the kids in their tracks. When he made it over to them he said in a calmer tone, relieved, "You know better than to walk away from us like that."

The kids got very quiet as they looked at their father. Neither one of them dared to move.

"I'm sure you don't think it was such a bad idea that I bought them light-up sneakers after all," Claudia said, still panting from running behind him.

Tino couldn't agree more. The four of them kept walking but stayed together this time. Lucas's left shoe light was faltering.

"What's wrong with Lucas's sneaker?" Claudia asked.

The boy stopped when he heard his name. Tino crouched down next to him, adjusted the laces, and tapped his knuckle on the bottom of the heel where the darned lights were.

"It must be the battery. I'll take a look at it when we get to Barcelona," he said.

They all headed for the exit. Tino was not up for another scare. He glanced at his watch; it was 7:30 pm.

"Let's go straight to the restaurant," he announced and took a few steps forward to ensure he made it to the Mosque's door first. He then turned around and waited for his family at the exit, paying close attention to each person behind them.

Lucas held the door of the Regadera restaurant open for his brother and parents. The place was not yet full, even though it was already nighttime. The tables were packed with tourists like them who preferred to dine earlier. The locals would start arriving around ten, when the Saturday night social life would take off and last well into the early hours of the following day. The young woman who had booked their table greeted them at the same counter where she and Tino had met earlier. Her hair was now down, and she was pleased with the change. As they met again, they exchanged knowing smiles that did not escape his wife's notice. The woman led them to their table and pulled out a chair for Claudia, who respectfully accepted the courtesy. Tino hung his backpack on the back of his chair, situated just behind the column, which blocked his view of the front door.

The waiter didn't take long to approach the table and offer them the menu. He served them water and left a basket of homemade bread and a bottle of extra virgin olive oil in the center of the table. The boys were the first to reach for it while Claudia resisted the temptation. The menu looked delicious. From his chair, Tino had a perfect view of the dishes being prepared in the kitchen. He loved the idea of the clear glass walls. They opted for the most original dishes, both in content and in fusion. The noise of surrounding conversations increased as the place filled up. The waiter came back to the table and stood next to Claudia, who began ordering food; first the kids' and then theirs. Tino stood up next to his chair, leaning forward to glance at the door.

"I'm going to the restroom. Lunch didn't agree with me," he said, putting his hand on his stomach. Claudia did not pay him much attention.

Another customer was walking toward the restrooms. Tino hurried to intercept him. The man gave way and they headed in the same direction.

In the narrow hallway, the two bathroom doors were easily identifiable by their respective symbols. The space was not well lit. At the end of it, some cardboard boxes partially blocked access to the back door used for day-to-day restaurant operations. He returned the favor and let the other customer go first to the gentlemen's restroom. When the man had entered and he was alone, Tino headed for the back door. He slid both locks open, slowly cracked the door, and stuck his head out. The automatic hinge attached to the top of the door to keep it closed put some tension on his neck. He pushed it open a little more and leaned his body out in order to take a better look outside.

It was a dark night and the restaurant's back alley was quiet. There were just a couple of trucks parked in front of other similar establishments. He went back in, closed the door, ripped a palm-sized piece of cardboard from the lid of an open box, and took a deep breath. He opened the service door again and this time stepped outside, hugging the exterior wall. He carefully pulled the door closed and placed the piece of cardboard at the height of the main lock to prevent it from latching. He made sure that the cardboard was secure and that it stuck out just enough that he would be able to pull it out upon his return.

It was almost nine o'clock and San Fernando Street was an example of what Isasa Avenue and its surroundings would soon become. Everyone was headed that way, where the best bars and restaurants in town could be found. The street's steep incline was not easily traversed, and there were more people walking down it than up like Tino. He ran as fast as he could, constantly keeping track of the time. He turned at the corner of Maese Luis and moved quickly to the other side of the road, stopping on Colon Street. The contrast between Colon and San Fernando was remarkable. There was no one on this narrow street. A few lights were on inside the apartments and some TVs were blaring. Tino scanned the facades on both sides, trying to remember the one he was looking for. He checked the time once again, only seven minutes had passed since he had left the restaurant. He walked briskly to the other corner of the block, which ended with a sharp right turn.

When he reached the intersection, he stood right in the middle of the street, then turned around and walked back to where he came from. He took a first step, a second one, and began to whistle the song *Guantanamera*. Tino paid close attention with every step and began to whistle louder as he made his way slowly down the street. To his left, a wide door with the number ten opened with a bang as he passed in front of it and a young couple appeared. The surprise made him pause for a few seconds. The couple started laughing at the lone "musician" as they walked away. He took another deep breath, resumed his tune, and continued his exploration. He had not fully taken another step when the next door—number 12—opened up. An outstretched arm grabbed Tino by his neck and dragged him inside.

The dark, enclosed entrance to the apartment doubled as a garage for an old white four-door Seat. Tino landed face down on its trunk and felt the pressure of what was, without question, the barrel of a gun on his back. He heard the door lock.

"What the fuck are you doing here?"

"You're getting old on me, Dean," Tino said with a mocking smile.

He turned around with his hands up, without moving away from the trunk of the car. After a few seconds, he made himself more comfortable and observed the gun that was pointed at him—a 9mm Spanish Star. Both men maintained eye contact, studying each other. Tino looked away only to check the time again, barely moving, as the Dean lowered his weapon while still pointing it at him. He half-opened the door and looked outside, waiting, searching. He locked it back up.

"I came alone."

"What's going on Tino? I didn't get all this gray hair for nothing, no need to sugarcoat it. But I've got to admit that sending you to do their dirty laundry is rather cruel. I didn't see it coming, I'm guessing this government doesn't want any loose ends. What's the order, accident or suicide?"

Despite the tension, the Dean seemed calm, convinced of what was bound to happen. Tino looked around, remembering the place.

"How can you think that? I'd never be part of such a thing," he answered, annoyed.

"Of course, now I get why they let me leave Cuba," he said surprised, as if talking to himself. "It's not the same killing me there as opposed to here. It makes sense," he stated with admiration. "I knew my time would come, just not so soon. I hope you learn from it Tino, for when your time comes."

The final phrase sounded like a sentencing, which Tino dismissed, although he understood his reasoning.

"Dean, I'm not doing anyone's bidding. They don't know I came to see you. I've never told a soul about this place."

"But you knew where to find me."

The Dean tightened his grip on the gun—he wanted to be ready in case he needed to use it. Tino was aware of this and tried to avoid any gesture or word that could trigger a misunderstanding.

"Cordova is impossible to forget. Don't you remember you brought me here after what went down on the Gran Via in Madrid? If it hadn't been for you, I'd have shot myself."

The reference was not lost on Dean.

"Right," he said and, dismissing the seriousness of the last phrase, he muttered to himself: "That Bulgarian guy almost screwed up the entire NATO operation."

Tino checked his watch again, but this time the sudden movement alarmed the other man.

"I'm here 'cause I need your help," he said, almost in a whisper.

The seriousness of Tino's expression concerned the Dean, who appeared to believe him. Tino lowered his gaze to the gun.

"Fuck off, Tino. Help you? I was about to shoot you. You know better than anyone how long it's been since I last heard that whistle. Bad habits die hard, dammit," he responded angrily. "I don't know how I can help you. I'm retired, remember?" he added with sarcasm.

"I don't have much time. Can we talk here?"

The Dean tucked the gun into his waistband and the tension eased. The two nacre plates on the pistol grip were visible and shined in the darkness. He pointed to the back of the entryway, behind the car, where there was a spacious white marble staircase with an iron handrail, lit by a simple lamp hanging from the ceiling.

"Claudia and the kids, all right?"

It was impossible for Tino to conceal his anxiety, especially hearing mention of his family. The Dean was fully aware that this was not a casual visit.

"I'm here with them. I left them at a restaurant between the Miraflores and Cordova bridges." He checked the time again. "I have ten minutes, Dean. I need you to take Claudia and the kids to Ourense and wait for me there."

"Ourense?" The Dean's disbelief was obvious. "Tino, you show up in my house in the middle of the night after going nearly three years without seeing each other and you ask me to—"

"Do you really think I'd ask you for something like this if it wasn't absolutely necessary? No one can take better care of my family than I can. You taught me that yourself."

"I don't know anyone in that town. How could you ask me to do this for you?"

"My oldest friend lives in Ourense, Sergio Hidalgo. I know you remember him—his father was the one who helped you expedite the papers for Spanish citizenship when they allowed you to leave Cuba."

"Yes, yes, I know who you mean. Does Sergio know we're going there?" The Dean did not wait for an answer, the look in Tino's eyes told him all he needed to know. "Of course he doesn't," he said, stating the obvious. "And what about you? What does he know? Everything?" he asked with distrust.

"Same thing my parents or Claudia know—that I work in State Security, that's it."

"Okay."

"Just make it to Ourense, you'll be safe there."

He pulled his gray iPhone 6 out of his pocket and held on tightly to the screen that displayed a picture of his children.

"Destroy it when I leave, please."

The Dean took his phone warily, for it was an omen of something worse yet to come. Something Tino wasn't telling him.

"Who's after you, Tino?"

"I don't know yet, that's why I need to get back to Cuba as soon as possible to find out who's trying to fuck me over."

The word *Cuba* upset the Dean.

"Rosa?" he asked with suspicion.

"Please, just go to Ourense. Don't take the highway and stay off the beaten track. Don't give anything away, zero contacts," Tino said in desperation, evading the question. "I hope you're still a good shot despite your retirement."

It came off as a joke, but it wasn't, and the old man knew it. Tino was dead serious, especially because his family was involved.

"I practice every week. You never know." They looked at each other, clearly the Dean had been right. "Just tell me one more thing, where are you coming from now?"

Tino checked the time again, five more minutes. He noticed the Dean had no intention of moving until he got his answer.

"From Ronda."

That wasn't the answer he was hoping for, but it was the one he'd feared.

"The story about the thief in Ronda is all over the news here."

"I had no choice. I had to scare them away to buy some time."

"You don't need to justify anything to me," he replied with indifference.

Tino hung his head, he was getting desperate because time was passing, and he couldn't plead with him anymore than he already had. The Dean leaned in close and put both hands on his face.

"I'll tell you the same thing I told you six years ago, when I brought you here after your first execution on the Gran Via." Tino looked up, his eyes fixed on his mentor. "In this business, when you get to the point of knowing more than you should, there are only two options: kill or be killed. There are countless examples and you're all too familiar with them."

The Dean let go of his face and headed for the door. He opened it and stepped onto the sidewalk where he waited for Tino, who quickly joined him.

"On the corner of Maese," he pointed in that direction, "two blocks down, there is an underground parking garage with two exits: Maese and San Pedro. There are four levels, I'll wait on the second one. I'm sure you're being tailed and you'll never shake them while you're in the city. Enter from Maese, leave Claudia and the kids with me, and exit on San Pedro, which takes you straight to the Andalusia Bridge and from there head to the highway."

Tino hugged him as if he were his father. It was a brief goodbye.

"Thank you, Dean. Someday you'll tell me how they let you take that gun out of Cuba and, better yet, how they let you bring it into Spain."

They both smiled mischievously.

"Didn't you hear what I just said? Too much information. If I told you, I'd have to kill you," he said mockingly. "Get a move on, see you in thirty."

The Dean went back inside his apartment and shut the door without looking back. Tino checked his watch. I'm on time, he thought, relieved, and started running as fast as he could.

The restaurant was nearly full. There was only one table left, but it certainly wouldn't be empty for long. Tino got to his table and—as the waiter finished clearing the plates—sat down as if it hadn't been almost twenty-five minutes since he'd left.

"Are you feeling better? Would you like me to box up your meal?" asked the waiter.

Tino looked at his still untouched plate, checked the time, and glanced at Claudia who looked worried and kept staring at him.

"Better yet, let's do dessert. Don't worry about my dinner, dessert and an espresso will do."

"As you wish."

"Bring us two crème brûlées for the four of us to share," Claudia said, emphasizing *four* as if it was the most important word in her order.

The waiter nodded and left with everything he had collected.

"It wasn't just a simple robbery last night, was it?" Claudia asked him.

Taken aback, Tino was quiet for a second.

"No," he confessed.

Claudia's face dropped. She grew pale hearing his answer.

"Are we in danger?" she said almost in tears.

Tino reached out and held her hand. He looked at her tenderly.

"Everything will be okay, don't worry."

Claudia pulled her hand back and awkwardly wiped away her tears, hiding her face so her kids wouldn't see her cry.

"I'm not going to ask you what last night was about. I love you and I always will, but my children cannot and will not be endangered because of your job. I'd better call my mom and get on a plane to Barcelona tonight so that you can fix whatever it is that's going on."

Tino listened to her calmly. The waiter returned with the desserts and placed them on the table along with four spoons. Each child took one. Tino scanned the surroundings and looked back at her.

"Nothing is going to happen to the kids, I'd never allow it. Trust me this one last time. It'll be over soon. You'll see."

Claudia looked him in the eye, wondering whether to believe him or not. She picked up a spoon and shared the dessert with the kids.

Outside the restaurant, several people were waiting patiently for their names to be called. Tino and his family walked toward their car that was parked nearby.

"Let me take a picture of you guys. Can I borrow your phone, Claudia?"

She leaned back on the car with one kid on either side of her as Tino composed the photo on her phone's screen. He wanted to capture the contrast between the night and the lights on the Cordova bridge. A silver Toyota Prius, across the street, next to the bridge, interrupted his concentration. He had already seen it on the highway, with two Caucasian men inside, but had not managed to identify their faces.

It must be them, he thought. The flash from the phone lit up the sidewalk.

"Let's take another, just in case," he insisted.

He zoomed in as much as possible on the Toyota's interior. The two men were talking without taking their eyes off him, but their faces were distorted, indecipherable, through the cell phone camera lens.

"Got it. Ready to go?" he asked his family.

The four of them got into the car. At that hour pedestrian traffic doubled that of cars, and Tino drove very slowly, glancing up at the rearview mirror to see if they were being followed by the Toyota. He stopped the Mercedes at a crosswalk. Nearing the end of the block he had the chance to switch to the opposite lane. He checked the time and his rearview mirror. The Toyota was two cars behind them. As the last person left the crosswalk, he laid on the gas and made a sharp U-turn to the left, much to the delight of Lucas and Rafael. Claudia only grew more worried.

"Put on your seatbelts," she commanded the children.

The Toyota copied the U-turn but without burning rubber. Tino knew there was not much he could do to shake them off in those traffic conditions, but at least he was confident that he'd made them. Now it was just a matter of reaching the parking garage where the Dean was waiting to throw them off for good.

Colón street was too narrow for a car like Tino's, and the roar of its diesel engine scared the passers-by away. The tires squealed as they scraped against the edge of the sidewalk. He spotted the corner of Maese Street about twenty yards away and jumped his car up onto the sidewalk, causing the pedestrians walking toward him to flee while cursing at him. The car was gaining speed and he got ready to make a right turn onto Maese to duck into the parking garage. The Toyota, lighter and narrower, was only a car away. Claudia watched Tino, she suspected something was about to happen, sensed it. She unbuckled her seatbelt and turned around to climb in the back with the boys.

"Not yet," Tino said as he put his right arm across her chest, reassuring her.

Claudia did as he said. The parking garage gate was wide open. A digital sign indicated that there were thirteen spots available. After crossing the entrance, Tino turned off the car lights and slowed down.

"Now, go sit with the kids," he told his wife with authority.

In less than two seconds she was in the backseat between her boys.

"Unfasten their seatbelts, the Dean is waiting for you. You need to go with him."

Claudia looked for him in the rearview mirror. Their eyes locked. Fear overwhelmed her. She knew that their farewell was inevitable, but she did not doubt Tino's reason for taking such a drastic action.

"I'm going back to Cuba, do everything the Dean says. He knows what to do. The only thing that matters now is that the three of you are safe. You can't go to Barcelona or get in touch with your family for now. Wait until I come for you."

"Then you—"

"I'll be ok."

The car began to descend almost vertically due to the slope of the ramp and they entered a dark, narrow spiral-shaped tunnel. The engine eased up and its sound became more hushed. Claudia unfastened the kid's seatbelts—they no longer seemed to be enjoying the ride and remained quiet and tense. The Mercedes made one final turn as it entered the second level. A brief flash of light signaled Tino and he stopped the car next to the Dean.

"Quickly, now!" he yelled and turned on the car lights.

Rafael was the first to jump out, followed by Claudia and Lucas. The Dean closed the door behind Lucas and hurried them to his car, parked in the first spot next to the landing between levels. In the rearview mirror Tino watched the flashes of light from his children's shoes as they got into the Dean's car. Just then, the spiral they had driven down began to light up. He floored the accelerator, searched for the San Pedro exit sign and headed toward it, tires squealing as he disappeared around the upward ramp. The Toyota Prius followed closely behind.

Madrid's Gran Via was not busy as usual, with no cars or pedestrians constantly coming and going amidst a deafening roar. It was Sunday, and still much too early for tourists and locals alike. An empty bus passed by, and a small cleaning truck sprayed the street with short, powerful jets of water while it collected the garbage from the previous night that was piled up along the sidewalk. Tino was driving down Gran Via at a low speed. He stopped at the traffic light on Silva Street, letting his eyes close as he waited. He needed to rest, even just for the couple of minutes it took for the light to change. Suddenly, Tino was startled awake as he felt the jets from the cleaning truck hit his car. The light was already green. He made a slow U-turn to stay on Gran Via and drove in the opposite direction.

He took his time driving. Gran Via descended slightly and curved to the right as it neared Valverde Street. He slowed down and put both hands on the wheel, looking up ahead at the wide clear window panes that made up the façade of the Gran Clavel restaurant two streets away. He changed to the middle lane, only a block away from the corner of Clavel Street. Restless, he adjusted his hands on the wheel and gave it a little gas, just enough to let the car coast as he crossed into the right lane. He let the car roll forward slowly until it hit the curb, which prevented the vehicle from going onto the sidewalk.

The heavy thud of tires hitting the curb almost knocked him off course, but Tino held the wheel firmly to maintain control. The few pedestrians walking along Gran Via's broad sidewalk at that early hour escaped being run over by a matter of seconds. Viktor still could not believe that Tino was ramming into his car, forcing him to drive directly into the façade of the Gran Clavel restaurant. He had not planned to execute Viktor there but had seized the opportunity when it presented itself. The slight downhill slope of Gran Via just before Clavel Street had allowed him to hide out of view of his target's rearview mirror. Clavel street was also blocked by a giant construction crane, preventing access to and from Gran Via. There was no maneuver that Viktor could pull off, and his brakes failed him in the rain.

The glass façade was completely shattered from the collision of the two cars. Tino's, a brand-new blue Peugeot 307, had crashed into the left side of the building. He could still feel the glass mixed with blood in his mouth, the stiffness in his neck, the rain pouring through the broken windows, and the people around the car yelling at him—although it was impossible to hear what they were saying over the infernal sound of the jammed car horn. To his right, Viktor's Ford was trapped under the heavy, opulent wooden door frame that had served as the main entrance and had collapsed onto the car's roof along with the rest of the front windows. The Bulgarian's head was tilted to his left, as if he were looking at Tino. It had smashed through the car window on impact and his neck appeared to be broken, as his head rested unnaturally against the edge of the door while blood trickled down his face and was slowly washed away in the rain.

The reflection of the Toyota Prius in the windows of the same restaurant abruptly interrupted Tino's memories. He looked for it in the rearview mirror. They had pulled over just fifteen feet away from him. He could make out their faces this time. With his right hand he reached for his backpack on the passenger seat, pulled out a tire iron, and placed it on his thigh. He waited. He took his foot off the brake and the car started to inch forward.

THE DROP

Terminal 4 in the Barajas airport welcomed the first passengers of the day. The Hertz parking lot was on the second floor of the building adjacent to the terminal where Iberia flights departed. Tino parked and checked the car one last time. He put the tire iron back where it belonged, grabbed his inseparable backpack, and headed for the exit. As he crossed the street that separated the buildings, he looked for the Toyota. It was stuck in traffic, near the crosswalk. The two men inside watched him, and he stared back with unflinching determination, openly exposing himself. When he made it to the terminal entrance, before passing through the automatic doors, he checked the boarding screen, focusing on the Iberia flight with the destination of Havana. He lifted his right hand as he entered the building, making the victory sign with his index and middle fingers, before hiding his index finger and leaving the middle one up as a final goodbye to his pursuers.

Chapter 4
Back Home

The cab headed down Paseo Street. With the car windows down, Tino could smell the ocean nearby. Exhaustion got the better of him at times. He hadn't slept for two nights in a row, but Havana's heat and humidity kept him awake. There isn't a single fucking cab with AC in Havana, he thought as he pulled his wallet out of his pocket.

The red light on the corner of Paseo and Línea forced the taxi to come to a stop, where Tino took the opportunity to pay and hop out of the car. El Potín, a coffee shop right on the corner, was already open so he went to the terrace and ordered a double Cuban espresso, no sugar. While he sipped it, he watched the white and green building on the corner of Línea and A, a block away from him. It stood tall, removed from the hustle and bustle of cars and pedestrian traffic around it.

The traffic in Havana was unlike that of any city he'd ever visited. There weren't many cars, though, as he crossed the street, Tino tried to maneuver around the ones expelling the most pollution. The capital was noisy because most of the vehicles were American cars from the 1950s that emitted more toxic gases than a hundred modern cars put together from any other capital in the world. He reached the deserted corner of Linea and A, slid his backpack off his back, and headed for the immaculate black marble staircase that led to the building's main entrance. A soldier in an olive green uniform greeted him with a military salute.

Natural light poured through the large glass windows into the medium-sized office made up of two wooden desks facing each other. There was an open Sony laptop on one of them and a closed rectangular metal case on the other. Tino came in and went straight to the desk with the case. He looked at it suspiciously, but did not touch it. He tossed his backpack down, unzipped it to pull out a set of keys, then hung it on the back of the chair. Once seated, he reached down to his left and opened the largest drawer. Taking out a Glock 43 9mm pistol, he released the magazine, counted the bullets, and checked to make sure there was one in the chamber. He put it back in the drawer and locked it.

"Hey! What are you doing here? What happened to your face?" asked a surprised Miguel from the doorway, in a mocking tone.

Miguel went over and greeted him with a firm handshake before taking a seat at his own desk, where he closed the laptop and took a sip of the coffee he was carrying.

"As expected, Claudia and I couldn't put up with each other 'til the end of the vacation," he answered dismissively. "What's this?" he asked, glancing over at the case.

Miguel set his coffee mug down and walked over to stand in front of the case next to Tino. He patted it a couple of times, resulting in a dull metallic sound, and made eye contact with Tino. An indecipherable expression spread across his face.

"*Etopodarok*," he said in terrible Russian.

"A gift?" Tino repeated suspiciously.

As his skeptical colleague watched, Miguel slid open the cylindrical locks on the box. Tino couldn't help but feel a bit anxious as he waited for its contents to be revealed. The first thing Miguel took out was a scope that he placed on the desk, followed by a state-of-the-art Russian AS Val rifle. He balanced the rifle up on his shoulder and aimed it at the horizon through the windows. Tino was unsure of the reason behind the present.

"Should we try it out today?" Miguel sounded like a kid with a new toy.

"Sure," he replied without much excitement. "Why the gift? Do you know?" he asked, intrigued.

Miguel lowered the rifle and put it back in the case along the scope. He went back to his chair while Tino waited for an answer.

"No idea, but we can ask our allies today," he said, putting air quotes around the word *allies*. "Your timing couldn't have been better. We have a meeting with the Russians at eleven."

The answer took Tino by surprise. He got up from his chair and walked over to him.

"Did they change the date?" The news made him a little uneasy. "The meeting was supposed to happen at the end of April, when you were back from your vacation."

Miguel shrugged his shoulders as he looked toward the back of the office where a thick frosted glass door blocked their view of the room behind it. Tino headed that way.

"Rosa's not there. She left early for meetings with the new minister, right here in the bunker."

Halfway between Rosa's office and Miguel's desk he paused for a moment, unsure of what to do next.

"I'm going for a coffee, want one?" he asked Miguel as he headed for the exit door. As he made it to the exit, he nearly ran into Rosa, who seemed unsurprised by Tino's unexpected visit. They stood facing each other.

"I figured you had come back. I've been calling your cell since Saturday, but you didn't pick up, so I assumed you were on your way back. Claudia, right?" Rosa headed for her office as she spoke. "Did Miguel tell you we've got a meeting at eleven?"

"He did." Tino followed her. "And why the date change?"

Rosa ignored the question and opened her door. She entered first, but let Tino follow her in. Rosa's L-shaped corner office had large windows along both sides. The smaller side faced the north and overlooked the vast sea stretching along the Malecón, Havana's famed esplanade, while the longer side looked out over the western city landscape. The curtains were all drawn back, allowing the soft morning light to filter in. That would not be the case at noon when it was impossible not to use them to block out the unrelenting afternoon sun. At the other end, a door led to the office's private bathroom and the rest of the wall was completely covered by metal filing cabinets, all properly locked and sealed.

Under the large west-facing window sat a leather couch, and two armchairs faced the desk. Tino closed the door behind him and sat on the couch to wait for Rosa, who had entered the restroom. The pictures on her desk were an invitation to peruse his boss's biography. They were mostly photos of her childhood, with her family, in various places and times. There were three photos in particular that were impossible to ignore, not only because of their prominence on the desk but also because of their content.

The first one showed a teenage Rosa standing next to her father in a large, beautiful garden in front of a mansion, captivated by a disheveled and bearded Fidel Castro in a relaxed pose and wearing his typical olive-green uniform. In the second, Rosa stood in a snow covered plain under a sign that read "Siberia." The third one showed the image of an older Rosa, with a serious face, standing next to her father and Castro during the Barcelona Olympic Games in 1992. Tino only knew the story behind the first photo. He was convinced that the other two, though seemingly obvious, had their own histories.

Rosa came out of the restroom and went to sit next to him; it was an unusual thing for her to do, and it had a relaxing effect on Tino.

"I hope the scratches on your face are Claudia's doing," she said sarcastically. "Tell me about the kids, I'm sure they're going to miss you. Where are they now?"

"Barcelona." He answered quickly to avoid giving further details. "I don't think they'll miss me much at the moment, they're having too much fun with their cousins. Maybe later on."

"You hadn't gone back to Spain since—"

"No." He answered before she could finish the sentence. "And since I was in Barajas for just a short while, I barely thought about that." He positioned himself on the couch in a way that blocked Rosa's view of the ocean. "So, are we still on for the meeting in Moscow at the end of the month, or will we handle all of our pending business today?"

His boss stood up and approached the window behind her desk. She gazed out at the ocean, enjoying the view.

"I don't think I'll go to Spain when they 'let me go.' Which, by the looks of it, seems like it will happen sooner than I expected," she said.

Tino leapt up and hurried to her side. The woman opened the window wide letting in the city noise and the sea breeze that was only perceptible at such a height. He leaned his body forward as far as he could, just as she did.

"They'd have to be pretty stupid to do something like that. This minister hasn't even been in office a full month and doesn't have a damn clue about what we do here!"

"He doesn't know how to do what we do, but he does know that we handle sensitive information that can destabilize this government at any time. That's what they're afraid of, and I'm sure they're already looking for replacements."

They talked without looking at each other and their voices were barely audible as they got lost in the ambient noise.

"You think they already have someone in mind?" he asked.

Rosa was pensive, she kept looking at the ocean trying to find the answers that eluded her.

"You better believe it." With their bodies still leaning outwards, she turned to face him. "They're going to wait for the right time to pull me out, just like they did with the Dean. The thing is that back then, I was the only person capable of replacing him."

"But he made some mistakes that cost him his job," Tino countered.

"Right, we know that, but the objective was to get him out and they used those mistakes to justify it. And they'll do the same to me when they see fit. These people won't stop 'til they've done a thorough generational cleansing and I'm one of the last thorns in their side."

"What do you propose then?" he asked, puzzled.

"Nothing. For now, let's just watch each other's backs."

"Got it."

"One more thing, Vasily Serminov is coming to today's meeting. I need you up to date on everything you've got."

"Of course," he replied reflexively. "Hey, is this Vasily *the* Vasily?" he asked incredulously. "The head of the FSB? The one who studied with you at the KGB school? You've told me you two were good friends for a while."

The woman turned around to take a look at the picture from Siberia on her desk. Tino followed her gaze.

"And he's the one who took that photo," she added wistfully. "But today's meeting is not between friends." Her tone became more severe. "Vasily hasn't gone through the trouble of flying all the way here without a serious motive and, unfortunately, I can't even begin to guess what it is. Can you think of any reason for his visit?"

"No idea," he answered without hesitation. "When was the last time you saw each other?"

Rosa closed the window and went to sit in her chair by the desk as Tino returned to the couch.

"Many years ago," she answered evasively. "Let's see what they want and cooperate with them per the current state of affairs. I've got to get down to the bunker to finish up a meeting. I expect you there at eleven, okay?"

He nodded as he stood up to leave. He made it to the door and opened it.

"You didn't by any chance happen to run into the Dean in Spain, did you?" The question stopped him in his tracks and got the attention of Miguel, who heard her from his desk.

"No, I didn't see him." He slowly turned around to face her and their eyes met. "Anything else?"

It was not a random question. He was sure of it and couldn't afford to entertain any doubts.

"Shut the door," she replied without looking at him as she focused on the documents she was reading.

The small room had a battery of high-definition screens transmitting images from the exterior cameras that watched and scanned the surrounding area, including the building's large interior side yard that could also serve as access to a variety of vehicles if necessary. Sitting at the foot of the screens, a soldier in olive green saw Tino standing by the metal gate that surrounded the property. He looked at the camera with a smirk and the soldier recognized him right away. He pressed the button on the corner of his desk and the gate opened letting Tino into the courtyard.

Tino walked in slowly as he exchanged formal salutes with two plainclothes guards who constantly patrolled the perimeter of the mansion. Their Russian Udav pistols were just visible underneath their spotless white guayaberas. The landscaping in the courtyard was simple but very well cared for, made up mainly of ferns and short flowering bushes. The side corridor ended at what had once been the living quarters for the employees of the main house. The door opened and he went straight inside.

THE DROP

The AC in the small room was running on full blast. After making his way over to a walk-through metal detector next to an X-ray machine, he took off his watch, belt, and wallet and put them in a plastic basket which he placed on the machine belt. He passed through the metal detector and it made no sound. The basket was already bouncing against the end of the belt, but he didn't collect his belongings; he stood still, waiting. A soldier emerged from one of the two doors in front of him with an electronic scanner used to detect any miniature recording devices or bugs that could be camouflaged inside clothing or shoes. He automatically extended his arms and spread his legs as the soldier thoroughly swept his body with the device. Once finished, he disappeared behind the same door that he had come from. Tino grabbed the basket and put his wallet in his pocket, his Casio watch on his left wrist, as usual, and buckled his belt back in place. He left the basket on top of the X-ray machine and headed for the other door.

The room was in shadows with the only light coming from a rectangular clear glass window that overlooked the adjoining meeting room. Standing by the window, Rosa was very focused on what was going on in the other room. Tino joined her without interrupting and pulled the curtains all the way back for a better view. He was also interested to see what was happening. At times, he turned his gaze to the other two-way mirror on the opposite wall of the meeting room, parallel to theirs. In the room, eight people conversed amicably through their respective translators, all seated at a luxurious wooden table. Rosa extended her left hand and, without looking, reached for a panel with two switches. She pressed the one on top and raised the volume a little so that the both of them could better hear what was being said.

"Cheap politics," she commented with her eyes set on a grinning blue-eyed man in his fifties, dressed in a white guayabera. He was the most attractive one in the group. "Do you know what the bastard said to me today?"

She reached out again, this time to mute the volume and turn on the lights. It took him a couple of seconds to get used to the brightness. Meanwhile, Rosa had already sat down in one of the two chairs that made up the room's only furniture. He followed her and took the second chair.

"What did he say?" Tino asked, watching the door next to the window and hoping it wouldn't open just yet. "What you mentioned to me earlier, about your retirement?"

"That man doesn't have the balls to ask me that. He wanted to know if I was interested in selling my house because his son was getting married, and he was looking for someplace close to his. Of course, since I'm an old maid, he figures the house is on the market—but you know what? I would rather set it on fire than sell it to him." She took a deep breath to calm herself down before speaking again. "Hey, wouldn't Claudia want to buy it now that you're getting a divorce? I know she's never liked living in that Old Havana penthouse. I'd move into the staff quarters, and she'd have the rest of the place to herself. The house is big enough for all of us and she wouldn't see me at all, except for when she'd have to bury me."

Tino didn't know whether to laugh at the request or take her threat to burn the house down seriously. He knew her well enough to know she was capable of it.

"It'll be unlikely that you see Claudia back in Cuba. But a house like that, you can sell at any price you want," he told her.

"And why wouldn't she come back?" she asked, annoyed.

"Her whole family lives over there, and I was the reason she didn't move before. But now that the divorce is inevitable, and considering how bad things are getting here . . . I'd rather have my kids grow up over there."

"If everyone thought like you, this country would be empty," she said, concerned.

"I don't plan to ever leave and you know it, but for right now, I prefer they don't live in Cuba."

"What makes right now so different from the last ten years that you've worked in State Security?" she asked defiantly.

The door burst open interrupting their conversation. Tino concealed his relief and stood up quickly, followed shortly after by his boss. Three people came out of the adjoining room and headed for the exit door without acknowledging them. Finally, the man whom Rosa had been watching through the glass appeared and headed directly toward her, not without blocking Tino, who had already headed toward the meeting room. To Tino's surprise, the man took him by the arm so they could approach Rosa together.

"This must be Tino, right?" he asked her without taking his eyes off of him.

"That's right, Randy," Rosa answered, annoyed by the minister's unusual gesture of familiarity.

"I already know Miguel. I actually worked with his father for a while until he got sick," he said with forced compassion. "A great man, no doubt about it. So, you were the only one left for me to meet on Rosa's famous team. How was your vacation in Spain? I look forward to going there myself, but with so much work I don't know when I'll get the chance."

"It was all right," he said briefly.

"Rosa, we need to set up a lunch with all of us to exchange ideas. Tino and Miguel are the future of this department, and I want to be up to date on all the work they do."

"Of course. We'll set something up and let you know."

"Very good. Tino, can I have a couple of minutes alone with your boss?" he asked respectfully.

Tino nodded politely and the minister shook his hand goodbye.

"So, Rosita, have you thought of an amount for the house?" he inquired as he smoothed out his guayabera, his protruding belly didn't make it easy.

She did not reply right away. Her discomfort was evident. She pulled back a lock of gray hair that had fallen in front of her eyes.

"I've told you, Randy, the name is Rosa," she insisted, calmly but emphatically. "And no, I haven't thought of an amount because I won't sell the house it took my father so much effort to build."

Randy wasn't bothered by the scolding because he had called her that intentionally.

"All right, Rosa," he said, looking her straight in the eye and completely changing his casual attitude. "Just consider that I'm basically doing you a favor. You know that in the area where we live, selling your property to a third party is almost impossible unless the Minister of the Interior signs off on it," he said, with a pompous reference to himself. "I . . . or rather, my son," he clarified shamelessly, "will pay you market price. You don't want to miss out on money that will come in very handy when you retire."

Once again he tried to provoke her, but he didn't have the necessary skills to do so. Despite the fact that he was her immediate boss, Rosa had no respect for him, and he knew it.

"As for the Russians," he changed the subject trying to pull rank, "we ought to take good care of them and you have to go along with everything they ask of you."

"Have to? Since when are the Russians in charge here?" Randy remained quiet. "Back in the nineties, when the Russians quit on us, you were very young. You mostly cared about cheering loyally during the young communist league meetings and growing out your hair. But I, along with many others, had to adapt to living without them, and we succeeded. Thanks to us, you enjoy the post you have today."

"Times have changed," he grumbled in defense.

"But idiots haven't," Rosa scoffed.

Her answer was met with absolute silence. The man could not believe what he had just heard and tried to come up with a way to smooth things over.

"No one is denying your commitment to this country, Rosa. We're all well aware of it," he said, taking the pressure off the conversation. "No one can change your record, but we must protect ourselves from the United States, and the Russians are offering support."

"The impeachment against the American president is about to make it to Congress," she stated.

"Come on, Rosa," his reply was dripping with sarcasm, "even I know that if the impeachment makes it to the American Congress, we may be looking at another civil war. He's still supported by the majority over there, and they won't let it pass that easily."

Rosa was surprised by the comment and knew he was right but concealed her agreement.

"This American president won't lose the election," Randy declared. "Look at it as your final service to our country before retirement."

"Look, Randy, I'll tell you something that may someday serve you as advice because I don't think we'll have many more opportunities to speak to each other like this." She took a step forward and stood a few inches from his face, looking him straight in the eye: "The day I think I can't give my best, I'll leave on my own, without anyone asking me to do so." She took a step backward. "Yes, I'll work with them." He let out a sigh of relief. "But as far as *I* see fit." As soon as she finished her sentence, she left him alone, angry and powerless about her decision.

Tino was rearranging the eight chairs in the meeting room when he heard the door slam. As he turned around, he saw his boss leaning against the door, frozen, trying to contain her rage. He decided against talking to her and continued setting up the chairs, which were organized in a way that made the division between the two groups clear, with four chairs on each side of the table. Rosa checked both walls and confirmed that the two-way mirrors on either side of the room were covered by curtains. A soldier came in through the opposite door carrying a tray with eight bottles of water and crystal glasses. He placed it in the center of the table and exited through the same door.

"Did you turn off audio and video?" asked Rosa.

"Everything is off and unplugged. I didn't expect—"

"Don't worry about him," she interrupted, unwilling to talk about it.

Rosa felt a slight push on the door she was leaning against, and she opened it to let Miguel in. He noticed the state she was in but didn't venture to inquire about it.

"Vasily and his entourage are already here," he advised as he approached the table and occupied the last chair on the right side.

Rosa and Tino followed his lead. She sat in the first chair and Tino in the one next to it. The door in front of them opened but no one came in for a couple of seconds. Then, a slender young woman in her thirties appeared, she had very white skin and blonde hair. With a smile on her face, she quickly waved hello and went straight to the table. She sat across from Tino, who couldn't help but admire her beauty from that proximity. As Rosa stood up to wait for Vasily, the noise of her chair sliding backwards interrupted their exchange of glances. Miguel also stood up, followed by Tino. Vasily appeared in the doorway and immediately looked for Rosa. His messy white hair was a perfect match to his Cuban guayabera of the same color. He walked decisively toward her and gave her a warm hug. No words were exchanged. To his surprise, she broke the embrace first. Vasily briefly greeted Tino and Miguel with a handshake and everyone sat down.

"You're the same old Rosa, I see," he said in rusty Spanish with a Cuban accent. "This is Irina; she'll be my translator for the day."

"Did you come alone?" she asked, ignoring Irina.

"*Da*," he replied, and Irina automatically began interpreting. "My team is headed directly to Washington, and I wanted to come here first to see you all," he explained looking directly at Tino and Miguel.

"How long has it been? Thirty-one years since the last time you were in Cuba, if I'm not mistaken?" Rosa said, convinced she was right.

"April, 1989, for Gorbachev's visit to Cuba."

"Back when you were known as the KGB, or have you forgotten?"

The sarcastic reminder didn't bother Vasily—it was true, after all.

"Of course not, but what I do recall very well from that trip was the farewell party at your house. What a night that was! Do you know the story?" he asked Tino and Miguel, who didn't. "We were all happily celebrating the success of the trip, but Boris, the head of the KGB back then, really stole the show. He got so drunk that he decided he had to have, by any means necessary, a feather from one of the peacocks Rosa had in the garden. I don't know if she still has them, but those birds were untouchable."

"I don't. I didn't have time to take proper care of them, so I gave them away," she said smiling at the anecdote.

"Anyways, we were all drunk, but not like Boris, who finally threw himself on top of a peacock and grabbed onto it. Right away, Rosa took out her gun, put it to his temple, and said—"

"If you pluck a feather, I'll blow your brains out," she recalled proudly.

Tino and Miguel were amused by the story, convinced that their boss was very capable of what Vasily recounted.

"Can you imagine saying such a thing to the head of the KGB? It was thanks to the Dean, the most sensible drunk in the group, that the whole event didn't turn into a shootout. He put an end to the madness and took us to have soup at the only place in Havana where you could have a great meal while listening to fantastic music. It was called La Bodeguita—"

"Del Medio," Rosa interrupted. "That's right, and it's still in business. You can imagine, though, that in thirty years many other restaurants have opened that are just as good or even better."

"Of course, many things can be done in thirty years' time," the Russian added sarcastically.

Rosa understood what he actually meant, but she was not going to go down that road and wear herself out in a useless argument.

"OK, so what can we do for you? I don't believe that you came all the way here just to chat about peacocks and restaurants," she asked bluntly.

"Do for each other, to be exact," Vasily replied, prompting no reaction from her. "We've received confirmation that a compromising video of the current US president exists." Vasily leaned forward and rested his elbows on the table while the others remained motionless. "We must get our hands on that material by any means necessary. It's essential for Russia, and therefore, for Cuba"—he looked Rosa in the eye—"to preserve the current state of affairs with the United States for the remainder of this term and the next one if possible."

He did not expect an immediate response to his request, not only because it was quite unusual, but also because he knew Rosa well enough to know she didn't appreciate that kind of imposition. She smiled slightly. Tino and Miguel remained serious, not uttering a word.

"I believe your request is four years overdue, Vasily," she said undaunted. "If this were the former administration, with which we had weekly contacts, it would've been plausible that such material could have fallen into our hands." Rosa glanced at her subordinates and looked back at Vasily. "Nowadays, we hardly sit at the same table. And when we do, it is mainly to talk about those damn sonic attacks on the American embassy here in Havana. In an ideal world, we'd have it, and I certainly wish we did, but that's not the case. This American president may be the perfect Russian partner but that's definitely not true for Cuba, and you know it."

"That's precisely the point, Rosa. If we get that material, it will be beneficial for both Russia and Cuba."

"But with Russia calling the shots," interrupted Miguel to everyone's surprise.

Vasily waited for Rosa to reprimand her subordinate, but she did not give in and sat there in silence.

"This isn't the missile crisis anymore, kid," he told Miguel in a patronizing manner. "Decisions are no longer made unilaterally. Our governments jointly agree on what to do for our mutual benefit based on the intelligence we provide them. That's our duty."

Rosa's laughter paralyzed the serious meeting. They all stared at her, shocked by her unusual reaction.

"Honestly Vasily, I don't know how you've managed to survive in this business for so long. It's a pity that we're not recording this conversation so you could listen to yourself later. You remind me so much of the Vasily I met in Siberia, the young communist militant ready to sacrifice himself for his country," she said ironically as she wiped away tears of laughter. "So"—she suddenly became very serious—"what duty are we talking about? The one that says we must blindly obey whatever comes from Moscow at any price so that later you can come and kick us in the ass whenever you feel like it, like you did in eighty-nine?"

Vasily couldn't contain himself, his face was flushed. He stood up and started to pace back and forth without looking at her. Irina maintained her smile but kept an eye on Vasily's every move behind her.

"We know they intend to send that material to Cuba," he said finally, carefully weighing his words.

"So, that's why you've gone to the trouble of coming all the way here," she announced, pleased with herself.

Vasily nodded and returned to his chair. He grabbed a bottle of water and drank it all. Irina took her own bottle along with a glass, filling it halfway up just to take a small sip.

"I don't know what makes you think we're involved in this operation, but, at any rate Vasily, I've already given you my answer," she concluded in defiance.

Rosa's apparent naivety drew a sort of childish smile out of Vasily.

"All right," he replied. "Can we assume that if the material were to *fall into your hands*," he made air quotes as he spoke, "you would share it with us, as you stated?"

"I'd have to consult with my government first," she answered succinctly.

The Russian's expression eased. As he listened to Rosa's answer his relief was inevitable, though, he tried his best to conceal it from her scrutinizing gaze.

"Of course."

"Do you have any idea what's on that video?" Tino asked suddenly, keeping a polite tone. "I mean, are we talking about something immoral, for instance? Given that this president is such a wild card."

"As far as we know, it's nothing like that," he explained solicitously. "I agree with you though, given such a character anything is possible."

Tino nodded in appreciation and the other man reciprocated the gesture. Rosa stood up putting an end to the meeting, and approached her old friend, who also stood up as he saw her coming his way. The others headed for their respective exit doors.

"Thank you for paying us a visit. You don't know how much I appreciate it." Rosa hugged Vasily, who wasn't sure of the true meaning behind her farewell. "Come on, I'll take you to La Bodeguita for old time's sake."

"I wish I could, but I'm heading to Washington as soon as I leave here."

"Next time, then." She headed for her exit and Vasily for his. Miguel had already left, but Tino waited for her in the doorway. "Vasily," she called to him as she turned around, "good luck in

Washington." A sly smile crossed her face as she exited, with Tino right behind her.

Vasily did not move, Rosa's smile had stuck with him as a final jab.

"Let's go. I'm positive she didn't even know the video existed. She doesn't have it, not yet at least. Now that they're aware of it, we must hurry," Vasily stated with confidence as he and Irina quickly exited.

Rosa was the first to enter the bunker's courtyard, and she stopped to wait for Tino and Miguel. She was upset and there was no denying it. Her jaw was tense and her hands jammed into her pockets. Not a good omen for her subordinates who chatted trying to delay making their way to where she was standing. One of the guards in plain clothes interrupted his usual route as he watched them approach their boss. The three of them started talking after making it halfway to their destination.

"It was clear that this meeting with Vasily wasn't going to be pleasant, but I never thought it would be so serious." She spoke in a quiet but firm voice as she exchanged glances with both of them. "Do either of you have anything to add before I get a call from the powers that be?"

"I don't," Miguel denied.

"Needless to say, neither do I," Tino added. "But I do have to agree with Vasily on something," his statement could not have come at a worse moment given Rosa and Miguel's evident annoyance. "We've got to get our hands on that video somehow." Tino made steady eye contact with Rosa. "And then we'll decide what's best for Cuba," he finished and waited for a response to his suggestion.

"Vasily is an old fox. He's convinced that someone wants to turn that video over to us and I don't doubt that for a second. Take the afternoon to think about how we can make it happen," Rosa ordered. "Let's meet first thing tomorrow in my office to discuss strategies."

The three agents walked toward the courtyard exit without another word.

Chapter 5
Friends

The shooting range was deserted. The sun was setting and the crisp green grass between the targets and the firing line contrasted with the blue of the sea in the distance. A narrow rectangular iron structure with a zinc roof served as a base for the shooters. Tino and Miguel looked through the scopes of the AS Val rifles to calibrate them. Next to them, on the floor, the metal cases were laid out, and between them stood a simple wooden table with a couple of chairs. An ice bucket chilling beer bottles rested on the table and Tinos' backpack was placed in one of the chairs.

"I'm ready," Miguel said as he stretched his body out on the ground to find the most comfortable position. "I'm going for the Dean's record. Was it four or six hundred-point shots?"

"Not even in your wildest dreams, Miguel," Tino mocked. "The Dean's record is ten consecutive hundred-point shots in thirty seconds," he rattled off.

"You're always defending him. Let me be happy just for one day, brother." Miguel protested.

Tino fired the first shot. The bullet sounded clean, interrupted only by the crash against the metal target on the other side of the pit. He checked his score using the scope.

"Eighty, not bad for your first try," his friend ridiculed.

Miguel inhaled, looked through the scope, pulled the trigger and briefly exhaled. He checked the score.

"Take that! Bullseye, a hundred points! Mark the first one down," he celebrated proudly.

Tino detached the scope from his rifle and stood up, leaving the gun on the floor. He placed the Glock he had on his right hip on the table next to the ice bucket and brought the scope to his eye. He looked for the target and confirmed Miguel's score.

"Well done. You've only got nine more to go in twenty seconds. Let's see it."

Miguel accepted the challenge and readjusted his body as his partner focused on the target. One shot followed the other in rapid succession. Tino smirked in silence after each bullet hit. After the ninth shot, he lowered the scope and stared at Miguel, who set the rifle aside, stood up angrily, and went straight for a beer. Tino did the same.

"Told you. The Dean's record is untouchable. Don't know how the hell he did it, but it's been twenty years and it's still there, undefeated," he taunted.

"Maybe it's just a legend, like so many of his stories," Miguel replied, defending himself as he sat down, popped the top off a beer using the bottle opener hanging from the bucket, and drank the whole thing in one go.

With his beer in his left hand, Tino put the backpack on the ground and turned the other chair around so that its back was facing Miguel.

"What's got you in such a bad mood?" he asked, a little surprised by his reaction but not reading too much into it.

"I'm quitting," Miguel replied with determination. "As soon as we've got the fucking video, I'm out."

Tino hid his immediate reaction. He needed to process Miguel's decision before replying. It didn't make sense to him, and it struck him as more of an emotional outburst than anything else.

"Does Rosa already know?" It was the first thing that he thought to ask.

"Of course not. I was gonna wait for you to come back from your vacation to tell her but given everything that's happened I'm moving things up. I'll tell her when we meet tomorrow. By the way, I'll need your help in Canada," he asked, "can you do it?"

"Yeah, of course. When?" Tino replied, willing to help him out.

"I'm leaving tomorrow afternoon."

"Give me until the weekend. I wanna make a couple of moves too and see what shakes out first," he added, with an ulterior motive in mind.

"No problem," Miguel agreed as he stood up to grab another beer. He took the cap off, tossed it into the bucket, and took a short sip. "Have you heard from Claudia and the kids? I'm guessing they're in Barcelona with Claudia's family."

Tino looked up to study Miguel. The glare from the sun was annoyingly bright and blinded him a little, so he took his hand to his forehead to see more clearly.

"Yes, I dropped them off there. Although, I'm sure they left the city and went off somewhere else, since they're all together," he answered evasively.

Miguel smiled.

"You're so lucky, my brother. Who would've thought that skinny kid from the Buena Vista neighborhood, who only had two pants and a pair of shoes to his name in college, would marry a Sureda heiress here in Cuba? Tino, man, excuse the indiscretion, we do go way back, but do you know how much dough she inherited?"

He became serious, although it wasn't the question that bothered him. He stood up and they faced each other.

"I don't know, Miguel. I was born with so little that everything seems a lot to me. I know that must sound ridiculous to you since you've always been so comfortable."

"Thanks to my dad. The only thing he did his whole life was work like a dog for this country, and now I can't even make a buck on the house. They say it's state property. So, what good was all his sacrifice?" he griped. "A new government came along after fifty years, and he wouldn't bend because he realized that they were up to no good. In return, they gave him the boot. And he died, alone and nostalgic for a country that turned its back on him. That's another reason why I'm quitting, I won't end up like him. This government's not going to screw me over."

"And what are you planning to do when you resign?" Tino asked, genuinely concerned. "There aren't many places where you can get the salary and privileges we've got."

"Charter boats," Miguel replied.

Tino let out a loud laugh, followed by another from Miguel.

"Oh man, you just reminded me of back when we were in college. We were always messing around!" Tino commented nostalgically. "Seriously, though, chartering boats?"

"I'm sure you remember Lucía Callejas, from our university."

"Of course, a neighbor of yours from Nuevo Vedado, another spoiled brat like you, all born with silver spoons in your mouths," he jabbed.

"That's her," confirmed Miguel dismissively. "Well, I ran into her in Montreal on my way to the strip club. Her father did give his *blessing*," he said as he air-quoted the word, "to the new government, but it came at a cost. He demanded that his daughter join an international company where she made good money, and lots of it. Lucía is now the co-owner of CUFLET and lives in Montreal, far away from all of this shit."

Tino remained unconvinced by his partner's career change. The story felt incomplete. He sensed there were some missing details he was still unaware of.

"You said it yourself, Miguel, we go way back, that's why I'm telling you I don't get it. I can't picture you sitting behind a desk taking orders from Lucía."

Miguel laughed mischievously as he heard the comment.

"Well, the thing is I explained it all backwards. That night I ran into Lucía, we ended up sleeping together. The idea of moving to Montreal came after."

"See, now I do believe that you would charter ships," Tino said confidently with a sly grin. "You should have started with that. You're cut from the same cloth. Congrats, my friend."

"Thanks, bud. It's funny what life has in store for you! One ends his cycle as a married man," he said, pointing his finger first at Tino and then to himself, finishing his thought, "and the other one starts it. If you need somewhere to go while you guys decide what to do with the penthouse, you can always stay with me."

"No, no. Don't worry about it, that won't be necessary. Claudia and the kids are staying in Spain for good."

Tino's comment took Miguel by surprise. "Really?" he asked incredulously. "And they'll stay in Barcelona?"

Remembering his family, Tino did not want to answer the question. At times he forgot what was keeping him away from them.

"You won't be able to cope with the distance, or all the time you'll miss with them." Miguel thought for a couple of seconds. "Why don't you take this opportunity and quit too? Let's get that video and leave as heroes. Once we have it in our hands, no one will care what we do," he concluded, enthusiastic about his plan.

"If we all leave Cuba, this country will never get out of the hole, Miguel," he lectured, convinced of his own words.

"Tino, there's no fixing this country and you know it. One by one, they've gotten rid of everyone from the old guard who didn't see eye to eye with their decisions. Look what they did to my father."

"Well, we can agree on that, but, are we going to hand over the country to them because of it? I can't give up that easily on what's taken me so much effort to earn, because no one has given me any help to get to where I'm at."

Miguel took it personally but didn't object—he knew Tino was right.

"And you're damn good at the job, you son of a bitch," he said with admiration.

"I don't know how to do anything else, and I don't want to," Tino admitted, looking at the rifle on the ground. "If I quit, my only choice is to move to Spain where I'll be dependent on Claudia's family, and I'm no good at that. And I'm not gonna win the lottery, so I've got to keep working. I'll find a way to be with my sons, don't you worry."

Miguel understood his decision.

"The divorce is to your benefit, after all."

"Why?" Tino asked, a little uneasy.

"Because having them outside of Cuba, you have one less problem to worry about if you keep working for these people."

Tino nodded as they clinked their beers. Night was falling and the sun had already disappeared behind the horizon. Both men picked their rifles up off the ground and packed them in their cases. Tino placed his on the table and collected the shells ejected by the firearms during their practice.

"Are you taking them?" he asked Miguel, offering him the shells, which he accepted. "Do you mind giving me a ride home and dropping the rifle at the office? I'm tired, it's been a really long day for me."

"Sure, man."

They checked their surroundings to make sure nothing was left behind. Tino put the Glock in his backpack, threw it on his back, and grabbed the ice bucket while Miguel carried the metal cases toward the exit of the shooting range.

A Hyundai Santa Fe pulled up at the corner of Obispo Street, in front of El Floridita restaurant. The strapping and well-dressed doorman, accustomed to handling the traffic out front to assist customers in entering the restaurant, looked at the car but couldn't make out anything inside of it. The black-tinted windows and the dark night made it impossible. The passenger's side door opened and Tino got out in one swift movement. The car sped off without yielding for the crosswalk, to the anger of many pedestrians. Tino put on his backpack, greeted the doorman, and headed east toward Old Havana through the crowded Obispo boulevard.

It was eight o'clock at night and the boulevard was still bustling. Depending on their nightlife preferences, tourists were walking down to the heart of Old Havana or up toward El Floridita. Locals also enjoyed themselves, but certainly with more shallow pockets. There was one thing however, that both tourists and locals did have in common—they were all being watched by obvious closed-circuit cameras and police, lots of them. Tino strolled along, enjoying the spontaneous, informal, and almost carnal interaction with other pedestrians like himself.

He reached the corner of Aguiar and Obispo. From there, he could see the penthouse where he lived, but as soon as he had started walking down the boulevard, he got the feeling that he was being followed. For the time being, he decided against going home. He kept on walking along Obispo until he made it to the Ambos Mundos Hotel. After passing through the lobby doors, he headed straight for the old-fashioned, gated elevator. He closed the door without waiting for the operator, pressed the last number on the panel and the heavy machine began to ascend. The elevator stopped at the top floor. Tino opened the iron door and entered a short corridor leading to the rooftop terrace where the night guard welcomed him with a strong handshake.

"What's up, Kike?" he asked with total familiarity.

"Same old, Tino. Do you want your usual table, or will you have a seat at the bar? It's still early so you can take your pick."

"No, I'll sit at my table," he answered as he scanned the deserted restaurant. "Do you have the iPad?"

"Yes. I'll bring it to your table," Kike replied and headed for the bar.

He thanked him and went to the corner of the rooftop, overlooking the intersection of Obispo and Mercaderes. The sight was spectacular. A perfect combination of the orange street lamps, the sea, and the colonial architecture. Tino inhaled deeply and sat down facing the only door with access to the rooftop. He put his backpack on the chair to his right, leaned against his thigh, and unzipped the outer pocket. He saw Kike approaching with the iPad and a drink.

"Here you are," the guard placed the device and a Cuba Libre on the table.

"Thanks, Kike," he replied, sipping the drink as he logged into the iPad and clicked on a file named "CCTV."

The guard took note of this and glanced toward the door.

"Anything I can help you with, Tino?"

"It's all right. No one would dare mess with me here while you're around. One look and you'd scare them off." He looked up to admire Kike's six-foot height and perfect physical shape. "Trust me, when the time comes—and hopefully it never does—you'll be my first call." He focused on the iPad and started checking the hotel's exterior cameras in the CCTV feed.

Kike understood that his presence was no longer required and went back to his strategic location by the entrance door, but now in a more alert state despite what Tino told him.

The CCTV feed did not show any faces that he recognized. Tino was mainly focusing on the hotel's access doors on Obispo and Mercaderes streets. He drank his Cuba Libre without taking his eyes off the iPad screen.

"May I sit down?"

Tino recognized the voice at once. He looked up. Irina smiled mischievously at him. She adjusted her mini skirt that barely covered her long white legs balanced atop a pair of very high heels in an intense black color. In her right hand, she carried a narrow rectangular purse covered in gemstones. Tino hesitated and made her wait, successfully concealing his annoyance at having been discovered. He stood up.

"Of course." He pointed to the chair in front of him.

Irina pulled the chair out and took a seat. Tino waved to the waiter and Kike approached them right away.

"Happy to be of service, my friend," he said with his eyes glued to Irina's plunging neckline that showed off almost her entire chest.

"Seven-year rum on the rocks, please," she flirted with the guard as she placed her purse on the table.

He walked away smiling and Tino enjoyed her boldness. Irina turned to look at him. He turned off the iPad and put it aside.

"What show are you watching?" the young woman asked, looking at the device.

Kike briefly interrupted their conversation as he put a drink in front of Irina along with a small plate of olives before turning around and walking away without saying a word.

"*Trotsky*," he answered daringly. "It's amazing what one can learn about history after such a long time, isn't it?"

"Absolutely." Irina sniffed the drink like a true connoisseur of Cuban rum and took a sip. "I'd love to have met someone as daring as Trotsky. The same thing will happen to you guys. Just give it ten years and you'll be hearing the stories about the Cuban Trotsky, Lenin, and Stalin."

"That soon?" he challenged her. He was certain she wouldn't resist answering and she knew it. Irina shot him a naughty grin.

"Sooner, I'd dare say," she answered carelessly, taking her eyes off him to look at the city. "If we believe that Vasily's predictions are right."

He remained pensive, waited for her to finish admiring the city and attempted to get some other reaction out of her.

"I thought you were leaving with him today."

"I was supposed to, but I asked him if I could take a couple days off."

"What an understanding boss," he smirked.

"Not exactly. It's not for my sake, it's for my father."

Tino was briefly silent.

"Where did you learn Spanish, Irina? Or rather, where did you learn Cuban?" he asked, intentionally changing the subject.

"Right here, at the School of Arts and Letters. Class of 2004."

Tino was genuinely surprised.

"Is that so? How strange we never bumped into each other. We weren't a large group of students back then."

"Yes, we did. Many times."

Tino was shocked. He couldn't place her from back in his college days.

"Maybe you're mistaking me for somebody else. It wouldn't be the first time that's happened."

"How could I forget the University of Havana's triathlon champion?"

The news was almost a slap in his face.

"We trained together, well, not just the two of us of course" she said flirtatiously, "but with the track and field team. That was my sport. The thing is that you only had eyes for your girlfriend at the time. What was her name? Laura?" she asked, pretending to guess.

Tino did not reply. He had no doubt that Irina knew her name perfectly well.

"No, I remember now, Claudia," she stated confidently.

"And she still is, well . . . was. We're getting divorced."

Now it was Irina's turn to be surprised.

"Really? What a coincidence! So am I."

"When are you going back to Moscow?" Tino asked, trying to put an end to the conversation about family.

"I don't know yet. I'm in no hurry unless you want to come with me. I can talk to my father and he'll send us a private plane as soon as tomorrow."

"Powerful, your father, isn't he? I guess you lived here because you were with him."

"That's right." Irina finished her drink, turned around and showed Kike the empty glass, she then looked back at him. "We lived in Havana for eight years. I love this city. I've always thought there is something truly special about it."

"You're not the only one who feels that way."

"But right now, it's like a sick grandmother. It needs help, don't you think?"

"Definitely," Tino replied with conviction.

Kike arrived with her rum but didn't say a word.

"My father, who is a sly old fox, says that the generation that rules Cuba now is similar to the one they called the useless fools."

Tino stayed quiet.

"Do you agree?" she inquired.

"I can see why your father would make such a comparison," he paused briefly, "but I don't agree. I wouldn't call them fools, but they are ignorant, shortsighted. They sold themselves as harmless sheep and that's how they made it into the government. And little by little they've done a cleansing to get rid of those who have started to question the change they so greatly promoted." Irina stared at him, weighing every word he said. "What they've kept of their promises are the same old slogans: 'Down with the blockade' and 'We are continuity,'" he said it in a low mocking voice. Irina smiled in complicity. "But in reality, the plans . . . well, to hell with them! And the people too! They always end up paying the consequences. These guys don't see themselves in power for just a short while. They've got Venezuela syndrome; they're here to stay, forever, if we let them. And they're willing to sell their souls to the devil himself for it," he concluded, giving Irina an incriminating look.

She was not bothered by the insinuation. She paid full attention to Tino, understanding that his point of view was right.

"If you think they're so bad, why do you protect them then?"

"Who says I'm protecting them?" he replied calmly. "I'm protecting Cuba, the average Cuban who has no fucking idea how the world works but needs a hand anyway. At least I can offer them that. In any case, I'm convinced this government won't last much longer."

"If anyone overhears you saying that you could get into some serious trouble," Irina responded in a sort of a threatening tone.

"Who's going to tell them? You?" Tino asked daringly.

"*Niet*. That's none of my business. You and my father would get along brilliantly."

"I'm sure."

Irina raised her glass, inviting him to a toast. Tino reciprocated and they drank without diverting their eyes from each other.

"Do you have a picture of your father?" Tino asked with some reservations.

"Let's exchange photos? I'll show you one of my father, and you show me one of Claudia?"

Tino's dare turned out to be a mistake, but he couldn't back out now. He reached for his wallet in his back pocket and showed her the only photo displayed in the plastic divider. It was an old picture, faded with time, and the faces were blurry in what appeared to be a wedding ceremony. Irina took a look with frustration. She opened her small purse and retrieved her cell phone. She passed by several pictures until she found one in particular. She flipped her phone around to face Tino, who couldn't help but tense up a bit as he saw the image. It showed Irina in the middle with the Russian president to her right and her father, Tino assumed, to her left.

"They've been friends since the KGB academy. When he was elected president for the second time, he asked my father to help him with, let's say, the more unpleasant affairs of his office," Irina said, putting her cell phone back in her purse.

"I see. Why are you doing this, then? I'm sure you don't need to put yourself at risk like this."

"I do it for the secrets. All of my life I've only heard whispers, conspiracies, secrets," she said, enjoying her words.

"But anyone can have secrets. You don't need this job of ours for that."

"True, but not just anyone can have *our* secrets," she emphasized.

Tino took a sip from his Cuba Libre. He wondered whether he would be capable of acting like her.

"At least you're lucky to have a choice."

"You could have one too," she said earnestly. "There's nothing in this world you couldn't have if you gave us the video. Anything you want," she insisted almost lustfully.

Irina had taken longer to make the offer than Tino had originally anticipated.

"I don't have that video," he replied confidently.

"And we know that," she stated in a patronizing manner, not believing him. "But I have no doubt you could get it very soon. Whoever is working for you in Washington has the video. We're certain of it. What's more, I can assure you that no one is going to touch your asset, and you'll be able to keep using him inside the American government. That is, if you don't retire with all the cash we'll be paying you."

"How much are we talking about?" Tino asked with apparent naivety.

"Give me a figure."

"Twenty million dollars."

"Done."

Tino smiled incredulously.

"I'm not so sure you have that kind of power."

Irina reached for her cell phone in her purse and started to press numbers as he watched her.

"*Babushka*," she said in Russian.

Tino grabbed her hand signaling for her to hang up. Irina agreed and ended the call.

"If I were to get the video, how do I get in touch with you? How will you send me the money?"

"I'm sure you have an account in Andorra for your European operations," she said as he nodded in confirmation. "As soon as you lay hands on the video, call me and we'll send you half," she instructed, showing him the back of her cell with her phone number. "Memorize it. We'll organize the drop then, as well as the payment of the second half."

Irina's happiness was evident, no matter how hard she tried to conceal it. Meanwhile Tino remained still, silent.

"Okay, all right. Let's do it."

"Bravo!" She said loudly disturbing the customers who had started to arrive. "The fortune Claudia inherited will be a joke compared to what you'll make."

He was not expecting Irina to bring up that subject, but it was just what he needed to finalize his plan.

"That's exactly why I want the cash. Claudia will be able to maintain her status with my money, not her family's. We could go and live anywhere in the world without depending on them."

"That's how it's done. Like a good old Cuban macho," she said mockingly.

Irina stood up and took a last sip of her drink.

"Time to celebrate. How about we go dancing? What did you think, that I was some boring Russian lady? I love *Chocolate* and his songs, especially 'Bajanda,'" she said seductively.

"Oh, I'm sure there is *absolutelynothing* boring about you," he emphasized. "Better to leave it for the next time we meet, though."

"If you insist," she said, annoyed by the rejection but trying not to show it.

She said goodbye with an almost contemptuous wave and turned around to leave, swinging her hips excessively and humming the song "Bajanda"as she headed for the door. She approached Kike, who was watching her every move, and kissed him on the cheek, then headed for the elevator. The guard glanced at Tino eager to chat but Tino, with a troubled expression on his face, had already returned to the iPad to check the hotel's CCTV.

Chapter 6
Rosa

The Seat traveled slowly through downtown Ourense. Pouring rain had not stopped locals from leaving their offices at lunch time and heading into the bars and restaurants that would be jam packed for at least an hour and a half. The Dean constantly scanned the car's surroundings through the rearview and two side mirrors. He squeezed the steering wheel tightly, fighting off exhaustion.

The city's cobblestone streets produced a monotonous rumble under the car, though not loud enough to wake Claudia and the children who were sleeping propped up against each other in the uncomfortable back seat. They were doubling back along the same route they had taken a while ago in the center of Ourense. Employees were already heading back to their offices and the crosswalks slowed down traffic. The delay permitted him to carefully examine his surroundings. His hands relaxed on the wheel, convinced that no one was following them. He took advantage of an opening in the crosswalk and sped off, heading out of the city center.

Rosa, seated behind her desk in the office, carefully read from a sheet of paper. Miguel, standing in front of the desk, was waiting for her patiently.

"May I come in?" Tino asked from the doorway.

He got no answer, but came in anyway and stood next to Miguel, patting him on the back to greet him.

"Why don't you answer your phone, Tino?" his boss inquired as she looked up to meet his eyes. "I'm going to tell you the same thing I told Miguel. I believe in random chance occurrences, but not in coincidences. This is the second fucking time this week that I've been taken for a fool. First Vasily, and now this." She showed him the paper with the FBI seal followed by a short paragraph.

Tino grabbed it, read it carefully, and handed it back to her.

"I think the FBI is just looking to fix their Montreal screw up. I'd have done the same thing," he said with absolute calm.

"That's exactly what I told her," Miguel backed him up. "It's just a random coincidence."

Their boss stared at them for a few seconds, her face still serious and tense. "And your cell phone, did you leave it in Spain or on the rooftop of the Ambos Mundos hotel?" she inquired.

"Battery's dead. I forgot to charge it last night," he answered, keeping his composure without giving in to the pressure.

"Fine. I'll accept that the meeting requested by our FBI friends is a 'random' coincidence," she announced sarcastically, staring at Miguel. "As soon as I give them the go-ahead, they'll take off from Miami. So we'll meet them in about an hour. Afterwards, we'll get together to go over the details of the plans you came up with. I'm sure some changes will be in order after our meeting with the FBI. You may leave now."

Rosa did not wait for them to exit and returned her focus to the document. Tino turned around headed for the door, while Miguel stayed behind and produced a letter-sized envelope from his back pocket.

"Rosa, I wanted to give you this."

"Later, when we meet," she replied without looking at him.

The steep street climbed high enough to mark a boundary between the outskirts of the city of Ourense and the endless surrounding forests. The Dean parked the car at the top of the hill, right behind the only other vehicle parked on that road and left the engine running. He looked through the rearview mirror, and then to his right at a bar that had its door open despite there being very few customers left inside. The tables on the sidewalk were also empty. Across the street, the thick woods began abruptly at the edge of the sidewalk, and a lamppost marked the start of a forest trail for amateur hikers in search of true wilderness. He looked down the street, at the end of the road there was a house slightly separated from the wild vegetation. Behind it sat a small garden running the width of the home, followed by an apple orchard, behind which the dense forest stretched out in all directions. On the front porch, a man played with a young boy of about four and a chocolate Labrador Retriever.

"Are we there yet?" Claudia asked, carefully distancing herself from the children so as not to wake them, as she searched for the Dean's eyes in the rearview mirror.

"Yes," he answered without taking his eyes off the man and the child.

"That's Sergio!" she exclaimed joyfully, keeping a low voice.

Claudia tried to open the car door on her side, but the lock would not budge. She shook the handle in frustration.

"Wait. Two more minutes, please," he said in a fatherly tone.

He didn't mean to sound imposing but it was impossible not to, and Claudia knew she had no choice but to obey him. She settled the children comfortably in their seats and enjoyed watching Sergio and his son play with their pet until the locks were suddenly lifted. Then, she opened the door, got out of the car and hurried down the street toward Sergio, who, upon realizing who she was, also ran to her—obviously puzzled and surprised.

Rosa, Tino and Miguel stood in silence, waiting in the bunker's meeting room. The door in front of them was closed, while the exit behind them remained open, along with curtains covering the two-way mirrors on either side of the room. On the center of the table, a tray held six bottles of water and the same number of glasses. Tino sat down first and poured himself a glass of water. The other two remained standing. A soldier in uniform poked his head through the door, right behind Rosa, and she immediately approached him. He whispered something in her ear that was imperceptible to Tino and Miguel. The soldier then left immediately, and Rosa shut the door.

"They're already here," she said as she walked to her chair. "Matt is coming, but no Ed, plus one special addition. You'll see."

She sat down enthusiastically while staring at Miguel, who held her gaze as he headed for his chair.

"Well, that's unexpected. Matt and Ed have been involved in the sonic attack investigations from the beginning," Tino said with concern as he turned his chair to face her. "Why did you agree to the meeting with such an imposition? We've been working with Ed all these years and we weren't far from recruiting him."

"That may be true, but when you see who it is you'll understand why. It's obvious that we can forget about Ed. That's how this business goes, and you both know it," she lectured them.

"I've made a lot of progress with my contact. He's not ready yet and so far his access is limited within the government, but he's got a good future. I'm certain of it," Miguel bragged.

Tino settled back into his seat and looked at him, waiting for him to finish.

"I asked Tino to come with me to Canada so we can work on him together. I think this contact can lead us to the video," he added for Tino's benefit, but his partner didn't seem satisfied with the explanation.

"Let's see what happens today first," concluded their boss, putting an end to the subject for the moment.

The door in front of them opened, giving way to two men properly dressed in suits and ties. The first one carried a leather briefcase. The two Cuban agents stood up while their boss remained seated.

"Good morning, Rosa. It's a pleasure to see you again," said the first man in Spanish as he extended his right hand.

"How are you doing Matt? It's great to have you back," she replied in English, smiling.

"Allow me to introduce you to David Silverman, special advisor to the president on Latin America affairs. But I'm sure you all already know that," he joked, seemingly amused by the obvious surprise on Tino's and Miguel's faces.

"First time in Cuba, David?" Rosa asked, already knowing the answer was yes.

Matt stepped aside so that David could make his introduction. Rosa extended her arm and firmly shook David's right hand. Matt took the opportunity to politely shake hands with Tino and Miguel and then headed to his seat, setting the briefcase on the floor, next to his chair.

"Yes, and hopefully not the last," replied David excitedly in perfect Spanish with a Cuban accent.

"Of course not! It's a great pleasure to have you here," Rosa flattered him a little. "Let me introduce you to Tino and Miguel."

The president's advisor approached them, greeted them in the same way, and sat down next to Matt. There was a brief silence as they sat facing each other.

"First of all, I'd like to apologize for what happened in Montreal," Matt began shyly.

"Speak up a little please, remember that I'm half deaf," Rosa interrupted him clumsily.

"Of course," Mark cleared his throat. "We didn't want to cancel the meeting at the last minute, but we had no choice because we were waiting to confirm the information we'll share with you today."

"I understand," Rosa said reluctantly. "What about Ed, is he coming back?" She knew her question was out of place, but that didn't bother her.

Matt wasn't expecting to be questioned by Rosa and was unsure of how to answer without upsetting her.

"Ed requested early retirement so he could go into the private sector. Better pay and less time away from home, as you can imagine."

"Smart move," she agreed, although unconvinced. "Very well, let's get started then."

"All right. We've already received the previously pending confirmation regarding the sonic attacks," Matt announced.

He placed the briefcase on the table, opened it and produced a small blue folder with the FBI logo in the center before closing it and putting it back on the floor. He took the folder and placed it on the table in front of Rosa, who did not so much as look at it.

"After suffering similar events," he continued his explanation without getting any reaction to his words, "the conclusion is that the equipment used is of Chinese origin. We have no doubts about it. You can verify this via the irrefutable data and references in the report."

Rosa slid the blue file, almost dismissively, to Tino who opened it and quickly skimmed through it.

"Matt, my government's position has not changed, and I'm sorry that you've come all the way here expecting something different from us. First, it was dissident elements within our young government, then Russia, and now China," she recounted in an almost mocking tone. "I'll accept this report in a personal capacity out of respect for the relationship we've built with you and Ed over the years, but that's it. After all, our leaders come and go, but we stay put."

Matt nodded in relief.

"Speaking of leaders," the American interrupted her, "the second reason for this practically informal visit is another subject, just as sensitive as the sonic attacks or even more so perhaps."

Miguel, who was carefully examining a page of the report, was the first one to react, closing the folder. Rosa and Tino waited calmly for him to finish his thought.

"It would be better for David to explain," Matt said, giving him the floor.

"Our government is willing to make some changes in its policy toward Cuba after the elections next November. This first presidential term has been very turbulent for reasons we're all aware of—"

"Sexual harassment, collusion, abuse of power," Rosa blurted out, intentionally interrupting him. "I never thought I'd see an American president with so many virtues," she added ironically.

"But in this next term, everything could be different. We could go back to the status quo of the previous administration, or even better," David concluded, attempting to conceal his anger at Rosa's interruption and mockery.

"In exchange for . . . ?" Tino asked, knowing they were all expecting the second part of David's explanation.

"A video," was the concise, quick response.

"You're in the wrong place. For filming permits you'll have to go to the Cuban Film Institute, which is in charge of such matters in Cuba."

David ignored Rosa's sarcastic joke, which made Tino and Miguel smile. He was not interested in arguing, but in controlling the conversation.

"We are aware there is a video that was shot illegally inside the White House. It does not compromise the president, but it could damage his candidacy for a second term. We're in the middle of election season and anything goes."

"Is it something personal in nature?" Miguel asked.

"No," Matt replied. "It's more circumstantial, but it could be misinterpreted or mishandled if it fell into the wrong hands."

"Does your family in Miami know you're here?" Rosa asked, dramatically altering the flow of their conversation.

David fell silent at the unexpected question about his family.

"Yes," he answered calmly. "I discussed it with my grandfather and he offered me his opinion, which I won't share here out of respect."

"Of course," she replied. "You should visit the synagogue in Vedado. It's been fully renovated and it's beautiful. I'm sure your grandfather would love to see it. As you know, he was one of its main supporters when it was founded. Matt can take you on the way to your embassy. It's not far from there."

"I'll try," he assured her, concealing the pride he felt as he heard her talk about his grandfather.

"I hope you don't miss the chance. You never know when you'll have another opportunity like this one," Rosa said, looking him in the eye. "Back to the subject at hand, why us?" she asked with distrust. "If that video really exists, it's more likely to land in the hands of the Chinese, or the Russians, or even the Israelis. Any one of them could afford to pay anything for goods like that."

"Maybe, but I think you all are the chosen ones. Otherwise, why else would Vasily himself have come to Cuba?"

Rosa leaned over the table without taking her eyes off him.

"Now listen here, I understand your political career started with this president, but Cuba and Russia have been allies for many years. Through ups and downs, but allies after all's said and done. Our relationship has visibly grown over the last four years and Vasily is part of that joint progress."

David smiled at the subtle scolding and kept quiet.

"Your president is a very good friend of the Russian leader. If you want to know why Vasily came to Cuba, perhaps he should ask him directly," she suggested defiantly.

"I don't think it's such a good idea to ask for favors of that magnitude right now."

"Because of the impeachment?" Rosa quipped. "Sometimes I think you Americans err on the side of being too politically correct."

"I couldn't agree more," David said.

Rosa remained pensive, considering his reply.

"I'll tell you what, in spite of the fact that this president doesn't exactly deserve our affection, considering all he's done against Cuba during his presidency, if that video were to fall into our hands, we'd give it to you."

The silence in the room was absolute.

"The reason for such a decision is a very selfish one and I'll tell you why," she continued. "We wish to resume the road to prosperity in the relationship between our two countries, for everyone's sake." Rosa looked David in the eye. "Especially ours, for Cubans on both shores," she concluded.

Tino and Miguel could not believe what they had heard but refrained from disagreeing.

"That's precisely what this is about, Rosa," said Matt, satisfied. "Cuba and the United States are destined to have a better relationship, and I can assure you the president will keep his word after the election. Perhaps his family will even decide to invest in Cuba. We know that there have been previous attempts that did not come to fruition. Although, I'm sure the interest is still there. Right, David?"

"I'll be the first one to advise him to do so. Cuba has a great future and America will be an exceptional ally. The first presidential term was about politics; the second one will be about making money," he quickly confirmed.

"More than the president already has?" asked Rosa incredulously.

"Why not?" David replied.

Everyone in the room smiled in satisfaction. Rosa stood up and they all followed her lead. David leaned over the table and grabbed the blue folder. He produced a pen from his jacket and wrote a phone number on the upper right corner.

"This is my private cell phone. You can call me when you have the video, or for any other matter you see fit."

The boss and her two agents remained silent, trying to ignore the blue file. Until Rosa swiftly picked it up. She walked to the door and opened it. The same soldier as before appeared with a box of CohibaSiglo VI cigars. Rosa handed him the folder, took the cigar box, and dismissed him by closing the door. Matt rushed over to her as if he were a child being given candy for the first time.

"Do you smoke, David?" Rosa asked.

"If we're talking about Cohibas..."

Matt placed the box on the table and opened it. He and David inhaled the aroma of the cigars and each took one, hiding them in their interior jacket pockets.

"Just one? Does your grandfather smoke?" Rosa reached into the box and took another one to hand to David.

"He's faithful to his Romeo y Julietas, but I know he'll appreciate one of these if I bring it to him," he replied.

"Here. I can't give you the whole box since that would nearly be breaking the embargo and we don't want you getting into any trouble," she joked.

"Thank you, Rosa," he acknowledged, brushing off the ironic remark. "It will make my grandfather happy. I'll smoke mine right after lunch," he said as he put away the second cigar.

"Since we're in the area, we'll have lunch at the Cohiba Hotel, and then I'll take David to the smoking lounge to have our cigars. We've got to celebrate this excellent news," Matt added excitedly.

"They've just reopened the place. I was there yesterday and it looks spectacular," Miguel commented.

Matt thanked him with a nod. Rosa interrupted their interaction, suddenly closing the box and sliding it down the table to Miguel, who immediately opened it and took a cigar to the tip of his nose, taking in the aroma.

"Very well, Rosa. We'll wait to hear from you then, hopefully sooner than later. The clock is ticking and we need to resolve this matter as quickly as possible," emphasized David.

Rosa extended her hand to say goodbye and so did he.

"I personally will let you know when we have the video. That's a promise."

While David said goodbye to the Cubans, Matt returned to the table to grab his briefcase and then waited for him in the doorway until the two of them left together.

The back porch at Sergio's house was well lit. Artificial light illuminated the small garden and reached as far as the beginning of the apple orchard that continued on into the darkness of the night. Rafael, Lucas, and Sergio's son played with the dog. They ran along the rows of tomato plants, and the colorful lights from their shoes attracted the animal, who tirelessly chased them. Sergio, Claudia, and the Dean were enjoying themselves at the table on the porch, snacking on chorizo, ham, and local cheeses, accompanied by a bottle of red wine.

"Now Claudia, you couldn't have found more discreet shoes for the boys?" Sergio asked without taking his eyes off the kids, concerned about his precious garden.

"Make fun all you want, but it's thanks to those shoes we were able to find the kids when we lost them at the Mosque in Cordova. So don't judge them too harshly. You ought to buy a pair for your son," she replied humorously.

"No, thank you," he immediately discarded the suggestion.

"Sergio, tell your wife not to work too hard on dinner. After two days on the road eating sandwiches any hot meal will do," Claudia assured him as she sipped her wine.

"Don't worry, she enjoys it." Sergio leaned forward to take a look through the backdoor to make sure his wife wasn't around to hear him. "It gives her a break from the kid. He's driving her crazy."

Sergio and Claudia shared a laugh while the Dean downed the rest of his wine.

"Don't you have anything stronger in there, Sergio?" he asked, holding up his empty glass.

"Not a thing, Dean, I'm out of Havana Club."

"How about that little bar on the corner? Quiet?" he asked, standing up. "I need to stretch my legs."

"It's fine, a local joint. Ask for Fermín, he's the owner, and tell him I sent you. These *gallegos* get a little bit weird about strangers, especially at night."

"No worries, I'll let him know."

Claudia was staring at the Dean, trying to figure out the real reason for his nighttime excursion, although she was convinced she wasn't going to.

"Don't take too long, dinner will be ready soon," Sergio warned him. "By the way, since you arrived here I've only known you as the Dean, but surely you have a name."

The old man nodded and paused by the two steps leading down to the garden. He hopped over them, landing next to the vegetable patch, and crouched down. The dog ran over to him right away. Claudia leaned forward awaiting his answer, she also was curious.

"It is a cute Labrador. What's its name?" he asked as he patted the dog's back.

"Eco," Sergio said, still holding out for an answer to his question.

"The name's Manuel, I'm Manuel," he said nostalgically, but in a steady tone. "It's been so long since anyone's called me that, that I could hardly recall it."

Just then, the children arrived and interrupted the brief moment between the Dean and the family pet. He stood up and headed toward the front door of the house, walking along the side of it that faced the forest.

Seated on top of Miguel's desk, Rosa watched as Tino took the Glock from his backpack and slid it out of its case to put it in the holster he carried on his waist. Next to her there was her cell phone and a small wireless speaker, playing back the conversation recorded a few minutes earlier between the Cubans and Americans. The volume was remarkably loud.

"Miguel's resignation is excellent news, don't you think?" Rosa asked, making sure her voice was lost among the dialogue of the recording.

Tino left his backpack on a chair and took a seat on top of his desk, like Rosa.

"I'd prefer it if he stayed, but you're the boss and I'm sure you've got your reasons," he replied in a quiet voice.

"I'm certain. It's the perfect situation so that you can become the head of this department when they have me retired."

"I doubt it," he said incredulously. "I don't have any family lineage, like Miguel. I'd never be entrusted with that responsibility. Besides, you yourself think they already have a candidate in mind."

"You think just anyone could handle this position?" she asked without really expecting an answer. "I was sure they'd convinced Miguel to be the chief of the department behind my back. They would've killed two birds with one stone; Miguel's expertise in this business, and a respectful nod to this country's historic generation, being the son of a deceased general."

"I think you're giving too much credit to this minister."

"And I think you're blinded by your friendship with Miguel. Don't underestimate them Tino, these people take no prisoners. They go all out. And if you don't believe it, just look at all the dramatic changes this government has made in almost every ministry. Right now, you're not a threat to them, that's why Miguel's resignation is excellent news. Finding and training someone who can take over this place will take me at least a couple of years, time enough for them to get to know you well, and you them. So that they trust you and make you my replacement. When that happens, I'll be able to retire in peace without having to watch my back because I know you'll protect me just as I have for the Dean since he left."

Tino was silent. He believed his boss but doubted her intentions and was trying to come up with a response that didn't compromise him. He stood up and walked to his chair, placed the backpack on the floor and sat down.

"Rosa, I really appreciate your confidence in me, but I don't see it happening. There's too much at stake within these four walls for them to give up appointing someone from their inner circle."

"How many of them do you think are willing to step into the muck we live in almost daily and do the things that are practically second nature to us?" she asked him, smiling maliciously. "Don't buy that show the minister put on in the bunker. We're a necessary evil that they have to live with because they have no choice. But there's a long way to go from that to actually digging around in this shit."

The recording of the conversation with Matt and David ended. Rosa grabbed her cell, put it in her pocket, and turned off the wireless speaker. She stood up and approached Tino's desk.

"What did you think of David?" Tino's voice returned to its natural tone.

"It's a shame he won't get to be a career politician. As soon as this president is done or kicked out, off he goes. He could've been very useful to us. Even though he's third generation, didn't you notice how proud he is of his Cuban roots."

"Very proud," he agreed. "He almost lost his composure when you told him about the synagogue."

"Well anyway, nothing we can do about it," she lamented. "Miguel already left for Canada. Is there anything that worries you about replacing him and working with his asset? These changes have to be handled delicately. They can easily backfire."

"No, not a thing. I just asked him for a couple of days to do some investigating on my end before we meet up. He'll arrange a meeting with his contact in the meanwhile."

"I don't need to tell you that it's vital that we get our hands on that video. Whoever succeeds will go down in history. We're talking about the most popular American president in the last fifty years, and the most unpopular in the rest of the world," she said enthusiastically.

"I wanted to ask you about that. Can you play the recording again? I want to discuss something David said with you."

Rosa took out her cell phone and placed it on Tino's desk. She collected the speaker from Miguel's cabinet, turned it on, and placed it next to her phone. She started the recording once again at the same loud volume.

"Do you really plan to give the video to the Americans?" he inquired anxiously in a low voice.

His boss walked toward her office as Tino watched her, puzzled. She came back holding the photo where she was standing with Castro and her father in Barcelona.

"This was the day," she said pointing to the picture, "that the Dean, my father, and I had arranged a meeting with a personal friend of Bill

Clinton, who was also in Barcelona for the Olympic Games. We had clear signals that when Clinton became president, his Cuba policy was going to be different, non-confrontational—the Cold War was over, after all. All of our reports predicted Clinton as the winner in the November election that year, and we let Fidel know. When it came time for the meeting, Fidel called it off unexpectedly, claiming that Clinton would never beat a sitting president with the Bush last name, and he was not going to waste his time on a cause that was over before it started." She paused briefly. "The rest is history."

Rosa returned to her office with the picture as Tino sat quietly, considering her anecdote. She came back with a small, heavy safe that had a combination lock. She sat back down on top of Miguel's desk and placed the metal safe next to her.

"This is my second and last chance to make history, and I won't blow it by leaving the final call to politicians, especially not the ones we have today. If we succeed, I'll be able to redeem myself for my mistake," she said triumphantly.

"I agree with you, it's our call, not the politicians'—but the end goal must always be what's in Cuba's best interest."

"And it is. I assure you that you'll be fulfilling the oath you took when you joined the intelligence agency."

"To protect Cuba," he quoted with vigor.

Rosa paused, not taking her eyes off him.

"We both want the same thing, Tino, but the means to achieve it have changed. My Revolution, the one I fought for, doesn't exist anymore. Now only the country remains, and you have the privileged ability to shape it, to build the future you want for your children."

"Who are you planning on giving the video to?" he asked anxiously.

"The Russians—"

"But—"

"Listen," she interrupted him, "you're a very good agent, I'd venture to say one of the best I've seen, but you still have a few years to go before you'll be able to understand my decision. American rulers will always be predictable, even under a sui generis president like Roman, and proof of that is right under our noses. You just need to consider who he sent to do his dirty laundry, an outsider like David."

"David is one of his most trusted advisors."

"That's exactly why," she stressed. "But David does not belong to the Deep State. Roman knows that the only ones who can remove him from power are those in the Deep State—in the shadow government made up by the likes of Matt, Ed, and hundreds more whom Roman doesn't have control over, not yet anyway. If he makes it to a second term, he might."

"So you don't think there's any possibility that he'll be impeached?" Tino asked.

"Well, it's not impossible. Democrats can take it to Congress, but, if they win, they'll be risking not having another guy in the White House for the next twenty years because the majority that supports Roman would never forgive them."

"Maybe... perhaps you're right," he admitted, convinced.

"Of course I am. America only has two sides and while they may take different paths depending on the president in charge, in the end they both have the same objectives: free elections and democracy. We both know that our government isn't interested in either. The Russians, on the other hand—and this is something I learned from Fidel—will always be unpredictable, indomitable, and it's better to have them as allies, at any price. I won't turn over the video to them, but Vasily will know it's in my hands. We're the highest bidder in this story and *I* call the shots," she emphasized.

"I'm not sure that's the best call given that, as Vasily said, the Russians won't want to get rid of the American president, and that's what you and I want for the good of Cuba, right?" He questioned her emphatically, but got no answer, so he continued: "We'll end up in the same place we are now. Open confrontation between America and Cuba with Russia blackmailing us for their support."

"You're forgetting one detail," his boss remarked defiantly.

"What's that?"

"By controlling the Russians, we control our government. We'd be able to carry on working without worrying that they'd just get rid of me whenever they please, and that you would be made the boss of all this without any setbacks. When you're in charge of the department you won't have to travel as much, and you'll be able to get your family back," she paused, "and protect them."

The recording of the meeting with Matt and David came to an end for the second time. Tino clenched his fist, controlling his anger over the fact that he wasn't able to respond. Rosa put her cell phone back in her pocket and started to spin the dial on the safe until she unlocked it. She took out a stamp and adjusted the date of the small metal numbers.

"What passport are you planning on taking?" she asked in an authoritarian tone, back to her regular voice.

"Costa Rican. I'll first travel to Europe before going to Canada to meet Miguel."

His boss took out the Costa Rican passport, looked for the page where Tino's picture was and checked the expiration date. She turned the pages slowly, paying attention to the various entry dates and stamps: Honduras, the United States, Portugal, Mexico, and Cuba. She stopped at a page, grabbed the stamp and pressed it down in a blank space.

"Do you have a pen?"

Tino went to his backpack and returned with a pen in hand.

"I'll put Sunday as your entry date for Cuba, ok?" She didn't wait for his answer and wrote the numbers. "I'll enter it in the immigration system right now so that you can leave tonight."

"Good, the sooner the better," he said and collected the pen Rosa had left on Miguel's desk. "I need to go to my place to get some winter clothes for when I land in Canada. Can I borrow the car?"

"The key should be on my desk, where Miguel left it. You can give it back when you return. I have the other set. Oh, and please, fill it up before dropping it off. Where will you catch a cab to the airport?"

"From the Riviera Hotel. I haven't used it in a while".

"Ok, leave the car at the corner of Calzada and A. That's not too far for either of us."

Tino nodded and headed to her office to get the car keys as she locked the safe and waited to give him a few final instructions.

"Bring me the video, trust me," she insisted.

"Do I have a choice?" Tino replied provocatively.

"No," was her unequivocal answer.

They stared at each other, with Rosa still holding on to Tino's Costa Rican passport. She smiled lightly, extended her hand and Tino took the passport.

"Ok, see you soon." And with that brief goodbye, he walked over to collect his backpack from his chair and headed for the exit without looking back.

The bar was half full and customers chatted with each other while enjoying the nightly soccer program on the TV. The Dean, seated at the corner of the bar next to the front door, drank his last sip of neat rum while keeping an eye on the mirror above the freezers in front of him.

"Can I get you another, Dean?"

"No, thanks, Fermín, I'm headed out," he answered with a sigh. As he stood up he placed a twenty-euro bill on the bar. "They're expecting me over at Sergio's for dinner."

"Wait, I'll bring you the change."

"Keep it. Just be sure to save me some of that rum from back home. You'll see me again tomorrow," he said with a wink.

He heard Fermín's laughter as he walked over to the door. Stopping by the doorway, he adjusted the gun in his waistband so that his jacket wouldn't be an obstacle should he need to use it.

The bright orange light from the tall lamp post practically illuminated the entire street but barely filtered into the woods. He walked out to the middle of the road and started down the hill toward Sergio's house.

Tino parked the Santa Fe Hyundai next to the first gas pump at the station, turned off the engine, and got out of the car. On the opposite side, the owner of a blue and white 1957 Chevrolet convertible in mint condition was proudly filling his tank. Along with everyone else in the area, Tino admired the car's sleek lines as he walked over to the cashier to pay for his gas. On his way back, he noticed the Chevy's admirers had started chatting with its owner. Tino listened to them, amused by their conversation as he waited for the tank to fill up.

Once full, he put the gas cap on and got into the car. He felt a sense of relief as he isolated himself in its dark, cold interior. He had just started the engine when the back passenger side door opened and closed in a matter of seconds, just enough time to allow Matt to sneak in. Tino turned around, surprised to see him. He looked totally different than he did when they met in the bunker. He glanced at the Glock 17 with a silencer that Matt had aimed directly at his stomach and stayed very still. The American leaned over, stretched out his left arm and, watching Tino very closely, removed the pistol from his hip. He settled back into his seat and took off his Industriales cap, identical to Tino's.

"I was about to come for you."

"Sure," said Matt unconvincingly.

"Come on, let's get out of here!" he ordered in English.

The Hyundai Santa Fe moved slowly through the gas station and took a right on Malecón Avenue.

"Go to the alley on A Street, I've only got five minutes," Matt told him as he checked the time on his watch.

The car with the two men drove along A Street. About twenty yards before reaching the corner of Calzada Avenue, Tino made a careful right turn and entered a discreet alley between two houses. Very slowly, he navigated around an improvised soccer game among neighborhood kids and paused before making the mandatory left turn onto Calzada Avenue. He parked the car, leaving the engine on, placed both hands on the steering wheel and looked at Matt in the rearview mirror.

"What the fuck is going on here, Tino? You didn't follow our agreement about the video. Did you give it to Vasily yesterday?" Matt questioned him angrily as he held on tightly to his gun.

"That's exactly what I want to know. They broke into our bungalow in the middle of the night, with my family inside, sleeping—my family!" he said, containing his rage. "You can bet that if I thought it had been you, we'd have opened fire on each other right here in the car," he replied resolutely.

"Our agreement was that you'd deliver the video to the media in London, and you did not," he claimed, still not believing him. "I've lost all communication with you since the weekend, and then you show up unexpectedly in Cuba, the day before the arrival of the FSB chief. There's only one conclusion I can draw here, Tino—you've changed your mind and you're going to fuck me over."

Matt checked the time again, but kept an eye on Tino, who was scanning their surroundings on the car's three mirrors.

"Matt, if that were true, you'd be on your way to the Guantanamo Naval Base right now, with a hood over your head. We don't have much time because people are going to start coming out of their homes and they'll be wondering what the hell we're doing here."

Matt's relief was evident. He knew Tino was right. He rested the arm that held the gun on his thigh, but kept it aimed at him.

"What happened to you in Europe?" he asked, still suspicious.

Tino turned around, resulting in a sudden reaction from Matt, who pushed the silencer against the back of the driver's seat.

"Easy, Matt, easy." He tried to calm him down as he raised his left hand. "Get out your phone. Look for the news from last Saturday about a dead thief in Ronda at Los Soles Inn."

The American hesitated. He pulled his phone out of the pocket of his jeans and raised it up to the same height as Tino's chest. His arm that was holding the gun rested on his thigh again. As he Googled it, he alternated between reading and keeping an eye on Tino.

"That's why I cut off all communication, got my family to safety, and returned to Cuba to find out who the hell is behind all this."

"You did the right thing. I'd have done the same," he admitted. "Washington is still hunting for whoever has the video. No one is safe, that's why it's key to expose them as soon as possible."

"And I will. As soon as I know who the traitor is," he informed him, adding a long pause.

"No, Tino, we can't wait any longer. The longer we wait, the bigger the chance that they find me out. Make it public, and then we'll catch the son of a bitch. Besides, the traitor is someone you guys are already involved with. Any idea who it might be?"

"Could be anybody. At this point I don't trust anyone, not even Pietro in Montreal. With his mafia past, who knows."

Matt smiled. "Pietro is making way too much money in Montreal to get involved in this situation and risk his parole. Last thing he wants is to go back to a US prison. Believe me if there's anyone we can trust now, it's him," he added in reassurance. "When the video goes public, it'll be easier for you to find out who the traitor is because someone will have to pay the price for what happens."

"Okay," Tino agreed.

The owner of the house to the left came over and stood in front of the car and boldly looked inside. The two men noticed his awkward presence and ignored the indiscreet but justified reaction. They both fell silent. Matt handed Tino his gun, removed the silencer from his own and put it in the pocket of his jeans. He wedged his pistol against his hip and adjusted his white T-shirt to fully cover the handle.

"When I saw you pulling into the gas station, I thought I was screwed."

Tino smiled with pride.

"Ed's exit worked out well. I hope he doesn't get into a lot of trouble," Tino said casually.

"What's going on, Tino? Are you going soft on me?" Matt asked jokingly. "Ed is necessary collateral damage. One less son of a bitch, and it's taken the pressure off us for a few days. We should take advantage of it."

"What about David, he isn't a problem for you?"

"Not at the moment," replied Matt confidently.

"Understood. Where did you leave your suit?" he asked, gesturing at his outfit with his chin. "I don't know how you manage to wear jeans under your pants."

"Habit. I hid the suit in the bathroom closet in the lobby at the Cohiba Hotel. It was the only place I had time to get to when I saw you approaching the gas station." He checked his watch. "I've got to go, David must be about to finish that cigar Rosa gave him, and I can't be missing with a stomachache forever," he joked. "Thank you for looking for me, Tino."

"Trust me, if you hadn't mentioned the Cohiba, I'd have done anything to see that you didn't make it back to the US alive."

"I know," he said with conviction as he put his Industriales cap back on his head. "How do we get in touch?"

"I'll find you."

Matt nodded and got out of the vehicle. He turned left at the end of the alley and hurried along Calzada Avenue.

Chapter 7
The Betrayal

Three of the four tables on the sidewalk in front of the bar were empty. From the fourth one, set right on the corner, Tino monitored the three perpendicular streets that converged there with one of them ending at Sergio's house. His backpack sat in the chair to his right and on the table were two used, empty plates with no cutlery, and a bottle of water which he sipped from now and then. Traffic was very scarce.

Fermín carried the last table over toward the bar's entrance. He watched Tino, who did not move from his spot on the corner.

"Would you like anything else?" he asked loudly to make sure he'd been heard.

Tino turned to politely decline, signaling no with his hand. Fermín approached him.

"Man, you've been sitting there for three hours. You can use the restroom. We don't charge for it."

"Thanks, that's very kind, but I'm okay," he smiled at the witty remark. "I'm expecting a friend and don't want him to get lost, so I'd rather wait for him out here," he tried to justify the obvious concern on his face.

"It's up to you," said a suspicious Fermín. "It will be dark soon and the cold is unpleasant. When you decide to come on in, bring the chair and the table so I won't have to get them myself."

"You got it. No problem, I'll take care of it."

Fermín returned to the table next to the bar's entrance, swiftly picked it up and took it inside.

Sergio was tinkering with the ropes supporting his tomato plants in the garden when he saw the Dean headed his way, coming out from the apple orchard. He looked exhausted.

"What happened to you, Dean? You got lost?" he asked, concerned.

The Dean was out of breath and took a couple of seconds to answer.

"I still think I'm forty, and when I got to the edge of the orchard I went on into the woods. It truly is a beautiful place, but hell, it will trick you! What a long walk!"

Sergio was amused by the old man's story.

"Say, Sergio, when does the apple harvest begin? These trees are full of flowers."

"Early summer. If you want, you can stay here and lend me a hand. I mean, if it's not too much effort for you," he mocked.

"C'mon cut me some slack. I'm in pretty good shape for a 73-year-old man."

"You didn't happen to run into any wild boars in the woods, did you? As soon as the sun starts setting they come out for food and I have to bring the dog inside. He'd love to hunt them, but if I let him go for it, they'd kill him."

"Wild boars out here, really?" The Dean crouched down to tighten his shoelace and the grip of his Star gun became visible under his T-shirt. "That would've been the last straw!" he exclaimed. When he stood up he saw the expression on Sergio's face—he was no longer enjoying the story.

It was then that he noticed his gun was showing. He adjusted his shirt to fully cover the pistol.

"Sergio, you've got nothing to worry about," he promised with a serious expression.

"Dean, Tino and I are like brothers, we've known each other since we were kids. If he sent his family here with you, I'm sure that was the best call. I'd have done the same. But I'll ask just one thing of you," Sergio said, staring in the direction of the gun on the Dean's hip. "The minute you realize we're in danger, you have to tell me, don't keep it from me. I don't care how bad it is, I just want to protect my family just as Tino's protecting his."

The Dean nodded and saw that Claudia was looking at them from the back doorway, intrigued by their conversation, so he spoke quickly in a low voice to prevent her from hearing him.

"You can count on it, but I'm sure nothing will happen."

Claudia left the porch and started to walk toward them, determined to find out what they were talking about. Before her imminent arrival, the old man turned around so that he stood with his back to her, and he faced Sergio.

"Tino will be back really soon, and everything will be fine. Let's keep her out of this. We don't need to worry her more than she already is," he whispered.

The Dean turned to look at Claudia, who was already in front of them.

"I'll be doing the cooking tonight. Any requests?" she asked.

"I'd love some *huevos estrellados*," Sergio answered enthusiastically. "I know your French fries are excellent too," he added, flattering her.

"Perfect. The kids also like that, so I won't have to cook two meals. After dinner I'd like for us to go to the bar," she said looking at the Dean, "just the two of us. I want to talk to you."

The Dean looked at Sergio. He knew he had no choice but to agree. "Of course."

"Great. Dinner's at nine."

Claudia walked away followed by the old man. Sergio stayed in his garden to keep working on his tomato ropes, but this time he paid more attention to his surroundings.

Tino carried the chair on his shoulder. He dropped it next to the empty table just inside the bar's entrance, and it was quickly occupied by two customers, adding to the crowd inside. Everyone was focused on the soccer program playing on the TV. He walked over the bar where Fermín was constantly pouring beers.

"The restroom, please?" he asked cheerfully.

"In the back, on the right. So, did your relative arrive? You seem pleased."

Tino toned down his smile.

"No, he didn't. I'm sure he'll be here tomorrow," he replied and headed for the restroom.

Fermín followed him with his eyes, dissatisfied by his answer. He would've liked to have gone after him, but customers were piling up in front of the bar.

Water poured out of the tap, filling up the sink. Tino looked at himself in the mirror, happy and isolated from the usual soccer conversations of a small group of men who were chatting away in the bathroom. Up to his left, hanging from a door that led to a closet, was his ubiquitous backpack. He stretched out his back and arms as far as he could, then turned off the tap and bent over until his face was completely submerged in the water that had accumulated in the sink. A few seconds later he took his head out, smoothed back his wet hair, and again looked at himself in the mirror. He pulled a bunch of paper towels from the dispenser and slowly dried his face as he tried to fix the hair that kept falling across his forehead. He threw the paper towels in the basket and slung his backpack on.

The noise in the bar was unbearable. Tino was moving slowly through the crowd as he was headed for the door when he saw Fermín waving him over. He changed course to approach Fermín and squeezed himself in between two customers at the bar.

"What is it? Did I forget to pay for something?" he asked, puzzled.

"No, it's just that relative you were expecting is here." Fermín pointed to the man on his right, who turned his stool so they were face to face.

Tino's expression became tense as he saw Miguel. The joy disappeared and he clenched his fist with all his strength. Miguel laughed and looked him in the eye defiantly, spreading his arms wide open.

"What, you don't want to give me a hug?" he asked sarcastically as he stood up.

Tino gave in and hugged him coldly while Fermín carefully examined both men's reactions. Tino looked at him.

"Thank you for everything," he said as he rushed toward the exit followed by Miguel.

Tino stood in the middle of the road, facing the opposite direction of Sergio's house. The strong, orange light from the lamppost along with the remaining glow of the quarter moon illuminated the street. Miguel stood in front of Tino with the same attitude he displayed in the bar, feeling like a winner.

"You didn't give us a choice, so I personally had to come to take care of you," he said confidently with a hint of arrogance in his voice.

"I really didn't see it coming," Tino said, frustrated. "I always thought the traitor would be Rosa. It's a good thing that your father isn't alive to see the piece of shit you've become. But don't worry, you'll have to face him when you see him up there, because today . . . today you're going to die," he threatened, filled with rage.

Miguel concealed his fear. He knew Tino had the skills to kill him as soon as he had the chance. He pulled a walkie-talkie out of his pants pocket, identical to the one the assailant had in Ronda.

"*Yagotov*," said Miguel on the radio, in Russian.

As he heard him speak, Tino was again taken aback.

"You're such an idiot—you chose the worst ally," he jeered. "Had you chosen the Americans, I'd at least have a little respect for you. Actually, I don't care whose side you're on or how many of you there are. You won't touch my family and I won't be giving you the video," he challenged him angrily.

Miguel glanced at the bar door that remained open. He could see and hear the customers inside. Taking three steps backward, he unholstered a modern 9mm Kalashnikov pistol from his waistband. He turned on a small flashlight connected to the bottom of the gun's barrel and kept his arm parallel to his body to disguise the weapon from any unexpected passerby.

"Drop the backpack and turn around," Miguel ordered.

Tino obeyed and let the bag slide down his back to the ground. He turned around to take the first step toward Sergio's house.

"No. Take the hiking path," commanded the traitor.

Tino stopped in his tracks. He was certain that Miguel was not aware of the Dean's presence. He took a left and walked over to the head of the trail, which started right below the lamppost. Miguel picked up the backpack from the ground, put it on his back, and followed Tino, staying a few paces behind him.

"*Uzheidu*," Miguel said in Russian as they entered the woods.

Tino weighed his options while they continued slowly down the dark path. Miguel lit the way from behind.

"The video isn't here. You're wasting your time," he tried to persuade him as he stopped in a small clearing.

Miguel stopped as well, keeping his distance, while he listened to what they were telling him through his tiny earpiece.

"Are they all there?" he asked. "Let me know when you're done and wait for me."

"They must be having dinner," Tino replied, although he knew Miguel wasn't talking to him. "I left the video hidden in Ronda, away from my family, envisioning something exactly like this going down."

"Perfect. Let's give them five minutes to finish up their dinner, and then we pick them up to leave for Ronda immediately."

"You know that's not gonna happen."

"We'll see." This time Miguel's tone was threatening.

"Don't you want to know who gave me the video?" Tino tried to distract him.

"At some point, I did, not anymore. When I deliver the video, I'll retire with the five million they're going to pay me, and then I'll disappear."

"You got played, *tovarich*," Tino said mockingly. "They offered me twenty. But don't feel bad about it because the Russians aren't going to let you live for too long anyway. Can I ask you something?" Tino said.

"Sure," he replied reluctantly.

"When did they recruit you?"

"Why torture yourself, Tino? If I tell you it'll only hurt you, trust me," he replied arrogantly, mocking Tino in return.

Tino remained silent, awaiting the answer and quickly trying to come up with a way to get out of the situation.

"Four years ago in Moscow, when we went over after the government changed hands."

"You broke so quickly!" Tino attempted to offend him but was unsuccessful. The traitor just smiled, unperturbed.

"Irina can be very persuasive, what can I say?" he confessed in a perverse tone. "If only you'd gone out partying that night in Havana, you'd know what I mean."

"Irina? All I had left to do was give her a pacifier and put her to bed after the story I told her."

Tino wanted to buy some time and tried to contain his anger having just learned the truth about his partner. He crouched down to tie his shoe, but all he could think about was lunging at the traitor to kill him. Miguel grabbed Tino's backpack and checked his belongings as he carefully listened in to what was being said through his earpiece. He pulled out a table knife and showed it to Tino.

"Seriously?" he scoffed, underestimating him.

"Give it to me and I'll show you how to use it," replied Tino defiantly.

Miguel held his breath. Put the knife back and threw the backpack into the forest.

"Get up. We're moving," he ordered.

Tino stood up, having decided he'd risk it and go for Miguel's neck the first chance he got. A leafy tree partially blocked the trail ahead, just past the clearing. He went around it as did Miguel, staying six feet behind him.

"Stop, motherfucker!" whispered the Dean, shoving his Star gun against Miguel's temple as soon as he had passed the tree.

Tino turned around at the sound of the old man's voice, overwhelmed with relief. He immediately approached Miguel and took his gun, radio, and earpiece, which he quickly pressed into his ear.

"Fuck, Dean. How did you know?" he asked in a whisper.

"Fermín called Sergio as soon as you left the bar to ask if we were still expecting another family member," he answered without taking his eyes off his prey. "I assumed you'd use the bar to wait a few hours and make sure you weren't being tailed before getting to the house."

"This bastard knows me too well and was waiting patiently," Tino said, angry at himself and staring at Miguel. "Fermín must have been alarmed by the look on my face when I saw this son of a bitch at the bar," he speculated, relieved. "Are the kids and everyone else all right? How many are we up against?"

"Don't worry, everyone is fine. Judging by the movements I noticed in the apple orchard behind the house, I think there are only two more of them. It won't be hard for you to track them since the grass isn't very high. You go ahead, I'll stay here with him. We're parallel to the house.

Go straight about a hundred yards through the woods and then turn right, you'll end up at the edge of the apple orchard."

Tino released the magazine from Miguel's pistol, counted the bullets, and popped it back in place. He cocked the gun carefully, trying not to make a sound, and disappeared into the forest, off the trail. The Dean grabbed the traitor by his neck and squeezed it as he forced him to stand up against the tree.

"One word and I blow your head off," he said, pointing the gun at him.

Tino ran as fast as the terrain and his instincts allowed. He continued in a straight line, parallel to the apple orchard, keeping in mind the distance the old man had given him. The earpiece was silent, but he was sure it wouldn't stay that way much longer. He turned right when he knew he had covered the hundred yards. He had made it to the end of the apple orchard. The moonlight helped his search for irregular shadows among the trees that would give away the presence of Miguel's men. He discovered the first shape positioned under artificial camouflage, right between the orchard and the forest a few yards in front of him, diagonal to the house. It gives him a good vantage point, he's got to be the last one, Tino thought. From there, not only could he see Sergio's entire house, but also a large stretch of the street in front of it.

He went back into the forest to position himself parallel to the assailant, careful to avoid moving any branch that would reveal his presence. Hidden by the thick vegetation between them, he stopped just fifteen feet away from the man. He crouched down, put the gun on the ground next to the tree in front of him. He grabbed a fallen branch and threw it to his left. He then looked at the man, waiting for a reaction. The noise was quiet, but perceptible. The assailant pulled back the dark green blanket that covered him and corrected his position, turning towards the sound and exposing a Russian Val rifle with a scope and silencer. He adjusted the night vision goggles and carefully examined the area where the sound had come from. He was completely camouflaged, including his face, which had been painted black. He returned to his original position and once again covered his body with the green tarp.

Tino's watch read nine thirty. He took it off and placed it next to the gun. He remained crouched down as he removed both shoes, his socks, and the T-shirt he was wearing. Lastly, he detached the flashlight from under the barrel of the gun. He filled both hands with mud and spread it across his arms, chest, and face in an attempt to camouflage his bare skin. The cold mud made his whole-body shiver, preparing him for what was next. With his shirt sleeve in the palm of his left hand, he placed the Kalashnikov's barrel on top of it, then closed his fist and wrapped his entire arm with the rest of the garment until the gun's grip became an extension of his hand.

He picked up his watch with his right hand and stood up. Catching a glimpse of the lights at Sergio's house, Tino thought of his children and Claudia. He tracked the moonlight and started to move very quietly towards the edge of the forest. He looked at the shadow of the first apple tree in front of him. With one large step he took shelter under the tree, hidden by its branches. He held his breath, and took another step towards the second tree. There was only one more until he reached the man hidden under the tarp, barely four feet in front of him.

The shooter's body was incredibly still; his controlled breathing made the steady movement under the blanket nearly imperceptible. Tino had reached the shooter's legs and only needed to make two more moves to be in the ideal location. He positioned his right leg next to the man's waist, and, putting all his weight on it, he swung the left one forward one as he dropped his watch on the blanket. The man spun around when he felt it hit his back, allowing Tino to meet him with a powerful, sharp blow to his ear that made him faint immediately.

He pushed the man's motionless body face down and quickly laid on the ground next to him. Taking off the night vision goggles, he recognized the man as one of his pursuers from Cordova. He put the goggles on and scanned his surroundings looking for the rest of Miguel's team. The Dean was right, he spotted just one more assailant with similar equipment and weapons in the middle of the orchard, fifty yards away from him, according to the automatic reading from his goggles. He was positioned right in the center of it, watching the house. Tino waited, motionless. He took off the goggles and laid down on top of the unconscious man to his right. While kneeling on his back, he grabbed the man's chin with his left hand and held the back of his head with his right. In one sharp movement, Tino snapped his neck.

The Dean tried not to appear impatient in front of Miguel. Leaning against the tree, he glanced at the house out of the corner of his eye, expecting a signal from Tino.

"Your record at the shooting range is history. I demolished it." Miguel was provoking him, but without raising his voice. "Don't believe me? Just ask your favorite student."

He crouched down and leaned against the tree, looking tired. His movement put the Dean on high alert.

"Get up and shut your mouth," the old man ordered in a low whisper.

"Give me a break, Dean, I'm tired."

"Tired, my ass. Stand up," he demanded.

He ignored the order and the Dean took a step closer, aiming at his head. Miguel launched forward, kicking off the tree with his foot, and pushed aside the Dean's arm that was holding the gun. He hit him square in his jaw, knocking him out cold. The old man fell against the tree with a thud and started bleeding from his forehead. Miguel approached him, took his gun, and ran off towards Sergio's house.

The moon was nearly hidden behind the clouds and it was difficult to make out anything in the apple orchard. Tino tucked the Kalashnikov pistol into his waistband, picked up the Val rifle, and put on the night vision goggles. He took wide steps from tree to tree looking for the position with the best vantage point. With each step, he scanned the interior of Sergio's house. He reached a tree with few branches and leaned against it as he slid the goggles off. After resting the rifle on his shoulder, he used the scope to begin looking for the second assailant. Holding his breath, he aimed straight at the head that was peeking out from under a green tarp. He fired a shot. The brief whistle of the bullet barely made a sound. Tino checked the scope. He pulled the trigger a second time.

He reached the assailant and crouched down beside him. Blood had spread over the entire tarp. Tino turned the body over and made sure he wasn't breathing, although that would have been nearly impossible after two head shots. He studied his face; he was the second man from the Toyota Prius. As he was rummaging through the man's pockets he heard a dog barking and noticed a faint glint of light coming from Sergio's house.

"Tino!" Miguel shouted.

He jumped up as soon as he heard Miguel yell from nearby. He ran towards the house but came to an abrupt stop between the orchard and the vegetable garden when he saw Miguel on Sergio's back porch, holding his son Lucas and pointing the Dean's pistol at his head.

"Drop the rifle and the pistol," Miguel said.

Tino stared at Lucas who was sobbing. The flashes of light from his shoes were an unbearable distraction. He looked for Claudia through the open door. She was holding Rafael and crying in anger. Sergio was next to her, and behind them stood Sergio's wife who was trying to console her son. He took the Kalahsnikov pistol from his waist, threw it aside, slid the rifle along the side of his body, leaning it against the ground, trying to hide it, and began walking towards the house.

"Not so fast, Tino."

The phrase stopped Tino in his tracks, who did not hesitate to obey.

"The rifle," Miguel demanded, pointing towards the forest. "Toss it."

"Everything is going to be okay, my love," he said tenderly, looking at Lucas and Claudia. He angrily threw the rifle towards the forest without taking his eyes off his son. He advanced to the two steps that separated the garden from the porch.

"The video. Now!" demanded Miguel, who was starting to lose it.

He pressed his body against the side of the house, next to the door, and held on to Lucas even more tightly. Tino climbed up one step.

"Tino, don't come any closer!" he shouted frantically.

"Do you want the video or not?" Tino asked in defiance.

"Tell me where it is. Sergio can get it," his ex-partner was very nervous, made obvious by the tremor in his voice and his body language.

"You have a gun to my son's head. I'm not taking risks with his life. *I* have the video. *I'll* give you the video, no one else," he insisted.

Tino got down on his knees and stretched his arm out to grab Lucas's left shoe. Miguel watched him suspiciously. Lucas lifted his leg reaching for his father's hand and Tino removed his shoe. He pulled out a short USB cable that was lodged inside the heel and popped the tip of it off. A light blue flash drive dangled from the end of the cable. He tossed the shoe aside.

"Here." Tino stretched out his arm with the flash drive in his fingertips. "Let Lucas go."

Miguel was hesitant. He took the gun in the same hand he was using to hold Lucas and forced him to take two steps forward. He snatched the drive from Tino's fingers before quickly returning to his position against the wall.

The hiss of the bullet grazed Tino's face as he jumped to cover Lucas and grab the pistol from Miguel. The traitor's body fell lifeless against the blood-stained wall, a gunshot wound cleanly piercing his temple. Tino snatched the gun from Miguel's hand, took Lucas in his arms, and ran into the house. He closed the door behind him and hugged Claudia and Rafael.

"He told me he'd come to help you. I was so stupid. I was the one who opened the door for him," Claudia stammered, crying.

Tino hugged her tightly. Sergio tried to get the dog to calm down as his wife headed to the bedroom with their son. The dog wouldn't stop barking at something outside. Without letting him go, Sergio cautiously opened the door.

"Dean!" Sergio exclaimed as he rushed out with his pet.

Tino reacted as he heard the old man's name and went over to him. His face covered in blood, his mentor was sitting on the ground by the last row of the garden with the Val rifle resting between his legs. They both offered to lift him up, but he refused.

"Is it true what this son of a bitch told me about beating my record at the shooting range?" he asked as he stood up, supporting himself on the rifle.

Tino laughed at the question while he and Sergio assisted the Dean.

"Of course not, Dean, that record is unbeatable," Tino replied.

The three men started to walk slowly toward the house accompanied by the dog, who kept barking and jumping between them.

Chapter 8
Starting Over

Seated at the bar, Tino watched the TV screen hanging in front of him while Pietro kept making noise walking from one side of the bar to the other, reorganizing tables and chairs, and clearing away empty bottles and glasses. Even though he was the only customer there, the television's loud volume competed with the outside noise coming in through the windows, which were closed. The racket was caused by asphalt pavers that had continued working through the night under a powerful white light.

"Are you sure he got the message?" Tino asked, turning around to meet Pietro's eyes. "I've been here for three hours and those guys out there are about to wrap up their shift."

Pietro walked to the inside of the bar, took a bottle of water out of the fridge under the wooden counter, and gulped it down.

"He knows you're here, but whether he comes or not, that's up to him. And don't worry about them. They work for me and they'll leave when I tell them to," he reassured him and glanced at the time on his watch. "It's two hours 'til sunrise. You've got time. Want a drink?"

"Water, please."

Pietro bent down and grabbed a bottle of water. He put it on the bar before returning to his chores. The front door opened and three construction workers came in. They were dressed in work clothes, including black-tinted plastic shields that hung from their helmets and covered their entire faces. Tino turned around to see who it was and, after doing so, turned right back to the TV. Two men joined Pietro at the back of the bar, and the third one headed in Tino's direction.

"Up for paving the street with me?" asked a familiar voice as the man took off his helmet and face shield and placed them on the bar.

Tino was surprised to see Matt, who was unrecognizable.

"Damn, without a suit and tie you always look like someone else."

Tino stood up to shake hands with Matt, who was trying to pull the heavy glove off his right hand.

"After all you've been through, I had to make sure there wouldn't be any surprises."

Matt, followed by Tino, headed to the back of the bar towards Pietro. As he saw them coming, the owner and the two workers walked over the front door to make sure it wouldn't open from the outside. Tino and Matt sat down at the last table in the back.

"Everything seems to be coming together, finally," said a relieved Tino. "Rosa took full responsibility for Miguel's alleged betrayal in working for *you guys,*" he emphasized as he shot a look at Matt.

"I still find it hard to believe that Rosa made that call."

"She'd rather quit than give the minister the pleasure of discharging her dishonorably. She got her way, on her own terms, and now we can all close this chapter that wasn't great for any of us."

"Don't let your guard down, the Russians won't forget so easily. They must be up to something if they haven't gone after you with everything they've got."

Tino intentionally ignored the comment.

"Over the last few days, I've been able to regroup and keep my head down."

"I'm glad. What about you? What are they planning to do with you?" he asked, trying to conceal his eagerness to find out the answer.

Tino looked at the TV screen that showed a CNN newscast announcing a breaking story.

"I think they're about to break the news," he said pointing at the TV. Matt also turned his attention to the screen.

A young and serious TV anchor was getting ready to read the update. She was visibly nervous, the makeup on her forehead slightly smudged with sweat.

"We have just received a note from the White House that reads as follows: 'President Roman Whitaker has decided to withdraw his candidacy for the Republican Party in this year's election due to personal reasons. He thanks all of his supporters across the nation and is confident in the strength of his party. President Whitaker will work tirelessly during the remaining months of his term to fulfill the pending commitments that were part of his presidential platform. God bless you all and God bless the United States of America.'"

The young anchor breathed a sigh of relief at the end of the quote and granted the floor to a group of late-night panelists ready to comment on the top story.

"Well done, Tino. Great job, really," Matt congratulated him sincerely. "We avoided the impeachment. As soon as the White House was asked to comment on the video, Roman had no choice but to drop out."

"Yes, it's worked out very well for you guys. But don't forget that this is also about Cuba. I kept my part of the bargain, now it's your turn to keep yours," the Cuban reminded him.

"You'll see. As soon as a new president is elected in November, things between our two countries will go back to the way they were before Roman, or even better, who knows."

"No matter who wins?" he asked with distrust.

"No matter who the next American president is. Trust me, *everyone* wanted to get rid of Roman," he emphasized. "You can do a lot of things as the president of the United States, even some that may be questionable, but you can't just say 'Fuck the Constitution.' That's never going to happen. It's not in our DNA."

"The Deep State in full force," he said almost mockingly.

"And what are you right now but your own version of the Deep State?" Matt questioned him without expecting an answer. "Believe me, it's impressive, very few people have the privilege to experience what you do, to be a part of what you're building."

"You're dreaming, Matt," Tino said evasively, although he could perfectly recall something similar that Rosa had said to him during their last conversation.

"No way. However, there is a drastic difference between your Deep State and ours. Your goal is quite personal, and I get it, but we work to protect our democracy—and I assure you there are more of us than you can imagine. Besides, working alone you wouldn't be able to accomplish much more than your job allows, for as long as you keep it.

Matt realized right away that his last remark had not gone over well.

"He still has a few months until November. A war . . . "

"The only thing Roman does in the White House these days is sleep," Matt interrupted him. "Tino, you and I will stay colleagues," he said ambiguously as he searched the inside pocket of his overalls under Tino's suspicious gaze. "Here. It's a gift. I'm sure you'll need it someday."

He stretched his arm across the table and handed him a narrow, transparent rectangular plastic case containing a small flash drive. Tino examined it curiously.

"What is it?"

"Did you get to see the video on the flash drive?" answered Matt with another question.

Tino shook his head, in what appeared to be an obvious answer for the both of them.

"You'd be amazed, there is enough to put Roman in prison for the rest of his life," he said pleased. "But as you can imagine, he's going to be pardoned, we can't send a sitting president to jail."

"No, of course not. You'd rather have him killed first," Tino said ironically.

"Anyways," replied Matt, almost agreeing with Tino, "you'll enjoy the story behind this gift that much more," he noted, pleased. "Remember when the Russian Minister of Foreign Affairs visited the White House?"

Tino nodded.

"Well, this was the visitor ID used by his translator. Since, on our side, we only had the President at that meeting . . . " he let the phrase linger for a few seconds to enjoy the anticipation on the Cuban's face. "Inside the metal clip holding the plastic is the camera we shot the video with. It's tiny, undetectable," he assured him proudly. "The software to use it and encrypt it is on the flash drive."

He was surprised by the gift. He knew it would have been nearly impossible to get that kind of technology on the black market.

"Well I'll be damned, in the end, Rosa was right," Tino muttered.

"How so?" Matt asked, intrigued.

"Because she kept insisting on not using digital technologies in our work. She was terrified of them because she thought they were going to screw her over."

"Maybe she was right," he mocked.

Tino smiled mischievously at the implication.

"Thanks, Matt. Thank you . . . really," he said in earnest.

"I hope it comes in handy, wherever you go."

Tino stared at Matt, hesitant to reply.

"They're making me the Station Chief, " they both remained silent, "in Venezuela."

Tino's confession came as a surprise to Matt, who couldn't conceal his uneasiness at the news. He looked regretfully at the gift he had given him a few seconds earlier, which Tino still held in his hands.

"Too much information, don't you think? They're compromising you by giving you the largest G2 intelligence station outside Havana," he replied with concern. "Not to mention what the place entails, and what they'll make you an accomplice to: drug trafficking, illegal agents all over the world, and, most dangerous of all, Hezbollah."

Matt was right and Tino knew it.

"I had no choice, Matt, I had to take it. If I hadn't, I wouldn't be here, and I don't even want to think what they'd have done to Claudia and the kids. Remember, she was also a witness to what happened in Galicia. That was the Cuban minister's order when I got back, and you know all too well that it didn't come from him. It was imposed by the Russians to sign either my pledge of loyalty or my death sentence."

"Of course, I understand," the American said laconically, still baffled by the news and at a loss for words. "I just hope the three of them stayed in Barcelona for good."

"Yes, that's exactly what they did, since the divorce is official now," he sighed in resignation. "It's for the best, though. They'll be safe there under the care of Claudia's family, isolated from all this shit."

"You know, if you want, you could just stay in Canada right now. I'd personally drive you to the FBI to get you and your family into the Witness Protection Program."

Tino studied him and couldn't help but show some interest. Matt didn't conceal his partial relief—he was hoping for a positive answer.

"In order to convince Claudia to do something like that, I'd have to tell her a lot of things about myself that I hope she never learns. And if I did tell her, you can be sure she wouldn't agree to it. I appreciate the offer, but no. I won't go into hiding in some godforsaken town in the middle of Nebraska, not without them."

Matt stood up, frustrated by Tino's answer, and started to adjust his overalls. He looked around for Pietro, who was chatting with the other two workers at the bar.

"I've got to get back to work," he said jokingly to disguise his annoyance.

Tino stood up and extended his hand. Matt returned the gesture right away.

"Take care, Tino. If you ever need me, you know how to reach me," he offered as a final goodbye.

He nodded. Matt walked over to the bar and picked up the rest of his uniform. He put on his helmet and face shield. Following Pietro and the other two workers he headed for the door, and just before leaving, right as he crossed the threshold, he turned around and scanned the back of the bar, but Tino was already gone.

About the Author

Iohamil Navarro Cuesta graduated with a degree in English Language and Literature from the University of Havana in 1994. He began his professional career as a production assistant at the Cuban Institute of Cinematographic Art and Industry. His debut as a feature film producer was the acclaimed movie "El Benny" by Jorge Luis Sánchez. Iohamil has produced Cuban and international films and TV series such as "Cuba Libre," "Yes," "Huracán Chamaco," "El Rey del Mundo," among others. "La Entrega" marks his debut as an author, and he is currently preparing to produce his first movie script.

About the Publisher

UriArte Publishing & Consulting
　Miami, Florida, U.S.A
　uriartepublishing@gmail.com
　https://www.facebook.com/share/hdVB98nhbzx22sCV
　Read more at uriartepublishing.com.

www.ingramcontent.com/pod-product-compliance
Lightning Source LLC
LaVergne TN
LVHW092050060526
838201LV00047B/1324